Marjorie's New Friend

Carolyn Wells

Contents

MARJORIE'S NEW FRIEND

BY

Carolyn Wells

CHAPTER I
A BOTHERSOME BAG

"Mother, are you there?"

"Yes, Marjorie; what is it, dear?"

"Nothing. I just wanted to know. Is Kitty there?"

"No; I'm alone, except for Baby Rosy. Are you bothered?"

"Yes, awfully. Please tell me the minute Kitty comes. I want to see her."

"Yes, dearie. I wish I could help you."

"Oh, I *wish* you could! You'd be just the one!"

This somewhat unintelligible conversation is explained by the fact that while Mrs. Maynard sat by a table in the large, well-lighted living-room, and Rosy Posy was playing near her on the floor, Marjorie was concealed behind a large folding screen in a distant corner.

The four Japanese panels of the screen were adjusted so that they enclosed the corner as a tiny room, and in it sat Marjorie, looking very much troubled, and staring blankly at a rather hopeless-looking mass of brocaded silk and light-green satin, on which she had been sewing. The more she looked at it, and the more she endeavored to pull it into shape, the more perplexed she became.

"I never saw such a thing!" she murmured, to herself. "You turn it straight, and then it's wrong side out,--and then you turn it back, and still it's wrong side out! I wish I could ask Mother about it!"

The exasperating silk affair was a fancy work-bag which Marjorie was trying to make for her mother's Christmas present. And that her mother should not know of the gift, which was to be a surprise, of course, Marjorie worked on it while sitting behind the screen. It was a most useful arrangement, for often Kitty, and, sometimes, even Kingdon, took refuge behind its concealing panels, when making or wrapping up gifts for each other that must not be seen until Christmas Day.

Indeed, at this hour, between dusk and dinner time, the screened off corner was rarely unoccupied.

It was a carefully-kept rule that no one was to intrude if any one else was in there, unless, of course, by invitation of the one in possession. Marjorie did not like to sew, and was not very adept at it, but she had tried very hard to make this bag neatly, that it might be presentable enough for her mother to carry when she went anywhere and carried her work.

So Midget had bought a lovely pattern of brocaded silk for the outside, and a dainty pale green satin for the lining. She had seamed up the two materials separately, and then had joined them at the top, thinking that when she turned them, the bag would be neatly lined, and ready for the introduction of a pretty ribbon that should gather it at the top. But, instead, when she sewed her two bags together, they did not turn into each other right at all. She had done her sewing with both bags wrong side out, thinking they would turn in such a way as to conceal all the seams. But instead of that, not only were all the seams on the outside, but only the wrong sides of the pretty materials showed, and turn and twist it as she would, Marjorie could not make it come right.

Her mother could have shown her where the trouble lay, but Marjorie couldn't consult her as to her own surprise, so she sat and stared at the exasperating bag until Kitty came.

"Come in here, Kit," called Midget, and Kitty carefully squeezed herself inside the screen.

"What's the matter, Mopsy? Oh, is it Mother's--"

"Sh!" said Marjorie warningly, for Kitty was apt to speak out thoughtlessly, and Mrs. Maynard was easily within hearing.

"I can't make it turn right," she whispered; "see if you can."

Kitty obligingly took the bag, but the more she turned and twisted it, the more obstinately it refused to get right side out.

"You've sewed it wrong," she whispered back.

"I know that,--but what's the way to sew it right. I can't see where I made the mistake."

"No, nor I. You'd think it would turn, wouldn't you?"

Kitty kept turning the bag, now brocaded side out, now lining side out, but always the seams were outside, and the right side of the materials invisible.

"I never saw anything so queer," said Kitty; "it's bewitched! Maybe King could help us."

Kingdon had just come in, so they called him to the consultation.

"It is queer," he said, after the situation was noiselessly explained to him. "It's just like my skatebag, that Mother made, only the seams of that don't show."

"Go get it, King," said Marjorie hopefully. "Maybe I can get this right then. Don't let Mother see it."

So King went for his skatebag, and with it stuffed inside his jacket, returned to his perplexed sisters.

"No; I don't see how she did it," declared Marjorie, at last, after a close inspection of the neatly-made bag, with all its seams properly out of sight, and its material and lining both showing their right sides. "I'll have to give it to her this way"

"You can't!" said Kitty, looking at the absurd thing.

"But what can I do, Kit? It's only a week till Christmas now, and I can't begin anything else for Mother. I've lots of things to finish yet."

"Here's Father," said Kitty, as she heard his voice outside; "perhaps he can fix it."

"Men don't know about fancy work," said Marjorie, but even as she spoke hope rose in her heart, for Mr. Maynard had often proved knowing in matters supposed to be outside his ken.

"Oh, Father, come in here, please; in behind the screen. You go out, King and Kitty, so there'll be room."

Those invited to leave did so, and Mr. Maynard came in and smiled at his eldest daughter's despairing face.

"What's the trouble, Mopsy midget? Oh, millinery? You don't expect me to hemstitch, do you? What's that you're making, a young sofa-cushion?"

"Don't speak so loud, Father. It's a Christmas present I'm making for Mother, and it won't go right. If you can't help me, I don't know what I'll do. I've tried every way, but it's always wrong side out!"

"What a hateful disposition it must have! But what *is* it?"

Marjorie put her lips to her father's ear, and whispered; "It's a bag; I mean it's meant to be one, for Mother to carry to sewing society. I can sew it well enough, but I can't make it get right side out!"

"Now, Mopsy, dear, you know I'd do anything in the world to help you that I possibly can; but I'm afraid this is a huckleberry above my persimmons!"

"But, Father, here's King's skatebag. Mother made it, and can't you see by that how it's to go?"

"H'm,--let me see. I suppose if I must pull you out of this slough of despond, I must. Now all these seams are turned in, and all yours are outside."

"Yes; and how can we get them inside? There's no place to turn them to."

Mr. Maynard examined both bags minutely.

"Aha!" he said at last; "do you know how they put the milk in the coconut, Marjorie?"

"No, sir."

"Well, neither do I. But I see a way to get these seams inside and let your pretty silks put their best face foremost. Have you a pair of scissors?"

"Yes, here they are."

Mr. Maynard deftly ripped a few stitches, leaving an opening of a couple of inches in one of the seams of the lining. Through this opening he carefully pulled the whole of both materials, thus reversing the whole thing. When it had all come through, he pulled and patted it smooth, and, behold! the bag was all as it should be, and there remained only the tiny opening he had ripped in the lining to be sewed up again.

"That you must cat-stitch, or whatever you call it," he said, "as neatly as you can. And it will never show, on a galloping horse on a dark night."

"Blindstitch, you mean," said Marjorie; "yes, I can do that. Oh, Father, how clever you are! How did you know how to do it?"

"Well, to be honest, I saw a similar place in the lining of the skate bag. So I concluded that was the most approved way to make bags. Can you finish it now?"

"Oh, yes; I've only to stitch a sort of casing and run a ribbon in for the strings. Thank you lots, Father dear. You always help me out. But I was afraid this was out of your line."

"It isn't exactly in my day's work, as a rule; but I'm always glad to assist a fair lady in distress. Any other orders, mademoiselle?"

"Not to-night, brave sir. But you might call in, any time you're passing."

"Suppose I should pop in when you're engaged on a token of regard and esteem for my noble self?"

"No danger! Your Christmas present is all done and put away. I had Mother's help on that."

"Well, then it's sure to be satisfactory. Then I will bid you adieu, trusting to meet you again at dinner."

"All right," said Marjorie, who had neatly; blindstitched the little ripped place, and was now making the casing for the ribbons.

By dinner time the bag was nearly done, and she went to the table with a light heart, knowing that she could finish her mother's present that evening.

"Who is the dinner for this year?" asked Mr. Maynard, as the family sat round their own dinner table.

"Oh, the Simpsons," said Marjorie, in a tone of decision. "You know Mr. Simpson is still in the hospital, and they're awfully poor."

It was the Maynards' habit to send, every Christmas, a generous dinner to some poor family in the town, and this year the children had decided on the Simpsons. In addition to the dinner, they always made up a box of toys, clothing, and gifts of all sorts. These were not always entirely new, but were none the less welcome for that.

"A large family, isn't it?" said Mr. Maynard.

"Loads of 'em," said King. "All ages and assorted sizes."

"Well, I'll give shoes and mittens all round, for my share. Mother, you must look out for the dinner and any necessities that they need. Children, you can make toys and candies for them! can't you?"

"Yes, indeed," said Marjorie; "we've lovely things planned. We're going to paste pictures on wood, and King is going to saw them up into picture-puzzles. And we're going to make scrap books, and dress dolls, and heaps of things."

"And when are you going to take these things to them?"

"I think we'd better take them the day before Christmas," said Mrs. Maynard. "Then Mrs. Simpson can prepare her turkey and such things over night if she wants to. I'm sure she'd like it better than to have all the things come upon her suddenly on Christmas morning."

"Yes, that's true," said Mr. Maynard. "And then we must find something to amuse ourselves all day Christmas."

"I rather guess we can!" said King. "We'll have our own tree Christmas morning, and Grandma and Uncle Steve are coming, and if there's snow, we'll have a sleigh-ride, and if there's ice, we'll have skating,--oh, I just love Christmas!"

"So do I," said Marjorie. "And we'll have greens all over the house, and wreaths tied with red ribbon,--"

"And mince pie and ice cream, both!" interrupted Kitty; "oh, won't it be gorgeous!"

"And then no school for a whole week!" said Marjorie, rapturously. "More than a week, for Christmas is on Thursday, so New Year's Day's on Thursday, too, and we have vacation on that Friday, too."

"But Christmas and New Year's Day don't come on the same day of the week this year, Marjorie," said her father.

"They don't! Why, Father, they *always* do! It isn't leap year, is it?"

"Ho, Mops, leap year doesn't matter," cried King. "Of course, they always come on the same day of the week. What do you mean, Father?"

"I mean just what I say; that Christmas Day and New Year's Day do not fall on the same day of the week this year."

"Why, Daddy, you're crazy!" said Marjorie, "Isn't Christmas coming on Thursday?"

"Yes, my child."

"Well, isn't New Year's Day the following Thursday?"

"Yes, but that's *next* year. New Year's Day of *this* year was nearly twelve months ago and was on Wednesday."

"Oh, Father, what a sell! of course I meant this *winter*."

"Well, you didn't say so. You said this *year*."

"It's a good joke," said King, thinking it over. "I'll fool the boys with it, at school."

The Maynards were a busy crowd during the short week that intervened before Christmas.

From Mr. Maynard, who was superintending plans for his own family and for many beneficiaries, down to the cook, who was making whole shelves full of marvelous dainties, everybody was hurrying and skurrying from morning till night.

The children had completed their gifts for their parents and for each other, and most of them were already tied in dainty tissue papers and holly ribbons awaiting the festal day.

Now they were making gifts for the poor family of Simpsons, and they seemed to enjoy it quite as much as when making the more costly presents for each other.

Marjorie came home from school at one o'clock, and as Mrs. Maynard had said she needn't practise her music any more until after the holidays, she had all her afternoons and the early part of the evenings to work at the Christmas things.

She was especially clever with scissors and paste, and made lovely scrap-books by cutting large double leaves of heavy brown paper. On these she pasted post-cards or other colored pictures, also little verses or stories cut from the papers. Eight of these sheets were tied together by a bright ribbon at the back, and made a scrap-book acceptable to any child. Then, Marjorie loved to dress paper dolls. She bought a dozen of the pretty ones that have movable arms and feet, and dressed them most picturesquely in crinkled paper and lace paper. She made little hats, cloaks and muffs for them, and the dainty array was a fine addition to the Simpson's box.

Kitty, too, made worsted balls for the Simpson babies, and little lace stockings, worked around with worsted, which were to be filled with candies.

With Mrs. Maynard's help, they dressed a doll for each Simpson girl, and King sawed out a picture puzzle for each Simpson boy.

Then, a few days before Christmas they all went to work and made candies. They loved to do this, and Mrs. Maynard thought home-made confectionery more wholesome than the bought kind. So they spent one afternoon, picking out nuts and seeding raisins, and making all possible beforehand preparations, and the next day they made the candy. As they wanted enough for their own family as well as the Simpsons, the quantity, when finished, was rather appalling.

Pan after pan of cream chocolates, coconut balls, caramels, cream dates, cream nuts, and chocolate-dipped dainties of many sorts filled the shelves in the cold pantry.

And Marjorie also made some old-fashioned molasses candy with peanuts in it, because it was a favorite with Uncle Steve.

The day before Christmas the children were all allowed to stay home from school, for in the morning they were to pack the Christmas box for the Simpsons and, in the afternoon, take it to them.

CHAPTER II
A WELCOME CHRISTMAS GIFT

The day before Christmas was a busy one in the Maynard household.

The delightful breakfast that Ellen sent to the table could scarcely be eaten, so busily talking were all the members of the family.

"Come home early, won't you, Father?" said Marjorie, as Mr. Maynard rose to go away to his business. "And don't forget to bring me that big holly-box I told you about."

"As I've only thirty-seven other things to remember, I won't forget that, chickadee. Any last orders, Helen?"

"No; only those I've already told you. Come home as early as you can, for there's lots to be done, and you know Steve and Grandma will arrive at six."

Away went Mr. Maynard, and then the children scattered to attend to their various duties.

Both James the gardener and Thomas the coachman were handy men of all work, and, superintended by Mrs. Maynard, they packed the more substantial portions of the Simpson's Christmas donations.

It took several large baskets to hold the dinner, for there was a big, fat turkey, a huge roast of beef, and also sausages and vegetables of many sorts.

Then other baskets held bread and pie and cake, and cranberry jelly and celery, and all the good things that go to make up a Christmassy sort of a feast. Another basket held nuts and raisins and oranges and figs, and in this was a big box of the candies the children had made. The baskets were all decked with evergreen and holly, and made an imposing looking row.

Meantime King and Midget and Kitty were packing into boxes the toys and pretty trifles that they had made or bought. They added many books and games of their own, which, though not quite new, were as good as new.

A barrel was packed full of clothing, mostly outgrown by the Maynard children, but containing, also, new warm caps, wraps and underwear for the little Simpsons.

Well, all the things together made a fair wagon-load, and when Mr. Maynard returned home about two o'clock that afternoon, he saw the well-filled and ever-green trimmed wagon on the drive, only waiting for his coming to have the horse put to its shafts.

"Hello, Maynard maids and men!" he cried, as he came in, laden with bundles, and found the children bustling about, getting ready to go.

"Oh, Father," exclaimed Kitty, "you do look so Santa Claus-y! What's in all those packages?"

"Mostly surprises for you to-morrow, Miss Curiosity; so you can scarcely expect to see in them now."

"I do love a bundly Christmas," said Marjorie. "I think half the fun is tying things up with holly ribbons, and sticking sprigs of holly in the knots."

"Well, are we all aboard now for the Simpsons?" asked her father, as he deposited his burdens in safe places.

"Yes, we'll get our hats, and start at once; come on, Kitty," and Marjorie danced away, drawing her slower sister along with her.

Nurse Nannie soon had little Rosamond ready, and the tot looked like a big snowball in her fleecy white coat and hood, and white leggings.

"Me go to Simpson's," she cried, in great excitement, and then Mrs. Maynard appeared, and they all crowded into the roomy station-wagon that could be made, at a pinch, to hold them all. James drove them, and Thomas followed with the wagon-load of gifts.

The visit was a total surprise to the Simpson family, and when the Maynards knocked vigorously at the shaky old door, half a dozen little faces looked wonderingly from the windows.

"What is it?" said Mrs. Simpson, coming to the door, with a baby in her arms, and other small children clinging to her dress.

"Merry Christmas!" cried Midget and King, who were ahead of the others. But the cry of "Merry Christmas" was repeated by all the Maynards, until an answering smile appeared on the faces of the Simpson family and most of them spoke up with a "Merry Christmas to you, too."

"We've brought you some Christmas cheer," said Mr. Maynard, as the whole six of them went in, thereby greatly crowding the small room where they were received. "Mr. Simpson is not well, yet, I understand."

"No, sir," said Mrs. Simpson. "They do say he'll be in the hospital for a month yet, and it's all I can do to keep the youngsters alive, let alone gettin' Christmas fixin's for 'em."

"That's what we thought," said Mr. Maynard, pleasantly; "and so my wife and children are bringing you some goodies to make a real Christmas feast for your little ones."

"Lord bless you, sir," said Mrs. Simpson, as the tears came to her eyes. "I didn't know how much I was missin' all the Christmas feelin', till I see you all come along, with your 'Merry Christmas,' and your evergreen trimmin's."

"Yes," said Mrs. Maynard, gently, "at this season, we should all have the 'Christmas feeling,' and though I'm sorry your husband can't be with you, I hope you and the children will have a happy day."

"What you got for us?" whispered a little Simpson, who was patting Mrs. Maynard's muff.

"Well, we'll soon show you." said Mr. Maynard, overhearing the child.

Then he opened the door and bade his two men bring in the things.

So James and Thomas brought them in, box after box and basket after basket, until the Simpsons were well-nigh speechless at the sight.

"How kin we pay for it, Ma?" said one of the boys, who was getting old enough to know what lack of funds meant.

"You're not to pay for it, my boy," said Mr. Maynard, "except by having a jolly, happy day to-morrow, and enjoying all the good things you find in these baskets." Then the Maynard children unwrapped some of the pretty things they had made, and gave them to the little Simpsons.

One little girl of about six received a doll with a cry of rapture, and held it close to her, as if she had never had a doll before. Then suddenly she said, "No, I'll give it to sister, she never had a doll. I did have one once, but a bad boy stole it."

"You're an unselfish little dear," cried Marjorie; "and here's another doll for you. There's one for each of you girls."

As there were four girls, this caused four outbursts of joy, and when Marjorie and Kitty saw the way the little girls loved the dollies, they felt more than repaid for the trouble it had been to dress them. The boys, too, were delighted with their gifts. Mr. Maynard had brought real boys' toys for them, such as small tool chests, and mechanical contrivances, not to mention trumpets and drums. And, indeed, the last-named ones needed no mention, for they were at once put to use and spoke for themselves.

"Land sakes, children! stop that hullabaloo-lam!" exclaimed Mrs. Simpson. "How can I thank these kind people if you keep up that noise! Indeed, I can't thank you, anyway," she added, as the drums were quiet for a moment. "It's so kind of you,--and so unexpected. We had almost nothing for,--for to-morrow's dinner, and I didn't know which way to turn."

Overcome by her emotion, Mrs. Simpson buried her face in her apron, but as Mrs. Maynard touched her shoulder and spoke to her gently, she looked up, smiling through her tears.

"I can't rightly thank you, ma'am," she went on, "but the Lord will bless you for your goodness. I'm to see Mr. Simpson for a few moments to-morrow, and when I tell him what you've done for us he'll have the happiest Christmas of us all, though his sufferings is awful. But he was heartsick because of our poor Christmas here at home, and the news will cure him of that, anyway."

"I put in some jelly and grapes especially for him," said Mrs. Maynard, smiling, though there were tears in her own eyes. "So you take them to him, and give him Christmas greetings from us. And now we must go, and you can begin at once to make ready your feast."

"Oh, yes, ma'am. And may all Christmas blessing's light on you and yours."

"Merry Christmas!" cried all the Maynards as they trooped out, and the good wish was echoed by the happy Simpsons.

"My!" said King, "it makes a fellow feel sober to see people as poor as that!"

"It does, my boy," said his father; "and it's a pleasure to help those who are truly worthy and deserving. Simpson is an honest, hard-working man, and I think we must keep an eye on the family until he's about again. And now, my hearties, we've done all we can for them for the present; so let's turn our attention to the celebration of the Maynard's Christmastide. Who wants to go to the station with me to meet Grandma and Uncle Steve?"

"I!" declared the four children, as with one voice.

"Yes, but you can't all go; and, too, there must be some of the nicest ones at home to greet the travellers as they enter. I think I'll decide the question myself. I'll take Kitty and King with me, and I'll leave my eldest and youngest daughters at home with Motherdy to receive the guests when they come."

Mr. Maynard's word was always law, and though Marjorie wanted to go, she thought, too, it would be fun to be at home and receive them when they come.

So they all separated as agreed, and Mrs. Maynard said they must make haste to get dressed for the company.

Marjorie wore a light green cashmere, with a white embroidered *guimpe*, which was one of her favorite frocks. Her hair was tied with big white bows, and a sprig of holly was tucked in at one side.

She flew down to the living-room, to find baby Rosamond and her mother already there. Rosy Posy was a Christmas baby indeed, all in white, with holly ribbons tying up her curls, and a holly sprig tied in the bow. The whole house was decorated with ropes and loops of evergreen, and stars and wreaths, with big red bows on them, were in the windows and over the doorways.

The delicious fragrance of the evergreens pervaded the house, and the wood fires burned cheerily. Mrs. Maynard, in her pretty rose-colored house gown, looked about with the satisfied feeling that everything was in readiness, and nothing had been forgotten.

At last a commotion was heard at the door, and Marjorie flew to open it. They all seemed to come in at once, and after an embrace from Grandma, Marjorie felt herself lifted up in Uncle Steve's strong arms.

"That's the last time, Midget," he said as he set her down again. "There's too much of you for me to toss about as I used to. My! what a big girl you are!"

"Toss me, Uncle Teve," said Rosy Posy, and she was immediately swung to Uncle Steve's shoulder.

"You're only a bit of thistle-down. I could toss you up in the sky, and you could sit on the edge of a star. How would you like that?"

"I'd ravver stay here," said Rosy Posy, nestling contentedly on her perch. "'Sides, I *must* be here for Kismus to-morrow."

"Oh, *is* Christmas to-morrow? How could I have forgotten that?"

"You didn't forget it, Uncle Steve," said Kitty, "for I see bundles sticking out of every one of your pockets!"

"Bless my soul! How odd! Santa Claus must have tucked them in, as I came through his street. Well, I'll put them away until to-morrow. They're of no use to-night."

"Put them in here, Steve," said Mrs. Maynard, opening a cupboard door, for there was a possibility that the good-natured gentleman might be persuaded to unwrap them at once.

Meantime Grandma was reviewing the small Maynards. Marjorie she had seen in the summer, but the others had been absent a longer time.

"You've all grown," she said, "but I do believe I like you just as well bigger."

"Good for you, Grandma!" cried King. "'Most everybody says, 'Why, how you've grown!' as if we had done something wrong."

"No, the more there is of my grandchildren, the more I have to love, so go right on growing. Marjorie, Molly and Stella sent love to you, and they also sent some little gifts which I will give you to-morrow."

The Maynards did not follow the custom of having their tree on Christmas eve.

Mrs. Maynard thought it unwise, because the children often became so excited over their gifts and their frolic that it was difficult for them to settle down to sleep until "all hours."

So it was the rule to go to bed rather early on Christmas eve, and have a long happy day to follow.

But the dinner, on the night before Christmas, always assumed a little of the coming festivities. On this occasion, the table was decked with holly and flowers, and the dishes were a little more elaborate and festive than usual.

"Ice cream, oh, goody!" exclaimed Kitty, as dessert appeared. Kitty's fondness for ice cream was a family joke, but all welcomed the little Santa Clauses made of orange ice, and carrying trees of pistache cream. After dinner a game of romps was allowed.

Mrs. Maynard, Grandma and Baby Rosy did not join in this, but went off by themselves, leaving the living-room to the more enthusiastic rompers.

"Fox and Geese" was a favorite game, and though there were scarcely enough of them to play it properly, yet that made it all the more fun, and Uncle Steve and Mr. Maynard seemed to be little, if any, older than Kingdon, as they scrambled about in the frolic. Then Kitty begged for just one round of Puss in the Corner.

Kingdon and Midget thought this rather a baby game, but they willingly deferred to Kitty's choice, and the grown up men were such foolish, funny pussies in their corners that everybody fell a-laughing, and the game broke up because they were too exhausted to play any more.

"Now to quiet down pleasantly, and then ho, for bed," said Mr. Maynard. So when they had recovered their breath, Mrs. Maynard and Grandma returned, Rosy Posy having already gone to her little crib. Mrs. Maynard sat at the piano, and they all gathered round and sang Christmas carols.

The children had clear, true voices, and the grown-ups sang really well, so it was sweet Christmas music that they made. They sang many of the old English carols, for the children had sung them every Christmas eve since they were old enough, and they knew them well.

Grandma loved to hear the music, and after it was over the three children were kindly but firmly requested to retire.

"We hate awfully to have you go, dear friends," said Mr. Maynard. "We shall be desolate, indeed, without your merry faces, but the time is ripe. It's nine o'clock, and Christmas morning comes apace. So flee, skip, skiddoo, vamoose, and exit! Hang up your stockings, and **perhaps** Santa Claus may observe them. But hasten, for I daresay he's already on his rounds."

Laughing at their father's nonsense, the children rather reluctantly backed out of the room and dawdled upstairs.

But there was still the fun of hanging up their stockings, and then, after that nothing more but to hurry to get to sleep that Christmas might come sooner.

Rosy Posy's tiny socks were already in place, and soon three more pairs of long, lank stockings were dangling emptily, and then, in a jiffy the Maynard children were all asleep, and Christmas Day was silently drawing nearer and nearer.

CHAPTER III
MERRY CHRISTMAS!

The sun waited just about as long as he could stand it on Christmas morning, and then he poked his yellow nose above the horizon to see what was going on. And everything that he saw was so merry and gay and full of Christmas spirit, that he pushed the rest of himself up, and beamed around in a glad smile of welcome and greeting. As he gave a flashing glance in at the Maynard girls' window, his rays struck Marjorie full in the face and wakened her at once. For a moment she blinked and winked and wondered what day it was. Then she remembered, and with one bound she was out of bed, and across the room to where Kitty was soundly sleeping.

It was a rule for the Maynard children never to waken one another, for Mrs. Maynard believed that people, both young and old, need all the sleep they can take, but Christmas morning was, of course, an exception, and patting Kitty rather vigorously on her shoulder, Marjorie called out, "Merry Christmas!"

"Who?" said Kitty, drowsily, rubbing her eyes, as she sat up. "Oh, Mops! you caught me! Merry Christmas, yourself! Let's go and catch King!"

Throwing on their dressing-gowns, and tucking their feet into bedroom slippers, they ran to their brother's room, but King, also huddled into a bath-robe, met them in the hall, and the gay greetings and laughter soon woke any one else in the house who might have been asleep. Nurse Nannie, with Rosy Posy, joined the group, and each clasping a pair of bulging, knobby stockings, flew to the nursery, where this Christmas morning ceremonial always took place.

A bright fire was blazing in the big fireplace, and in front of it, on a white fur rug, the four sat down, while Nannie hovered around, ready to inspect and admire, as she knew she would be called upon to do.

The big, light nursery was a delightful room, and with the morning sunshine, the shining yellow floor, white-painted woodwork, and bright fire-brasses, it seemed full of Christmas glow and warmth.

Grouped on the rug, the children immediately proceeded to the business of emptying their stockings, and as the various things were pulled out and exhibited, everybody oh'd and ah'd at everybody else, and they all began to nibble at candies, and at last Christmas had really begun.

The gifts in their stockings were always of a pretty, but trifling nature, as their more worth while presents were received later, from the tree.

But there were always lots of little toys and trinkets, and always oranges and nuts and candies, and always tin whistles and rattles, and other noise-producing contraptions, so that soon the four grew gay and noisy and Nurse was obliged to pick up Baby Rosamond, lest she should be inadvertently upset.

But perched in Nurse's lap, the little one waved a Christmas flag, and blew on a tiny tin trumpet, and quite made her share of the general hullaballoo. Marjorie had a new pencil-case, and some pretty handkerchiefs, and an inkstand, and a silver bangle, and a little diary, and some lovely hair-ribbons.

And King was rejoicing over a fountain pen, a pocket-knife, a silk muffler, a rubber-stamp outfit, and some new gloves.

Kitty had a little pocket-book, a silver shoe-buttoner, a blank-book, a pretty silk pincushion, and a bangle like Marjorie's.

Baby Rosy had dolls and toys, and what with the candies and other goodies, there was a distracting array of Christmas all about.

"And to think the day has scarcely begun!" said Marjorie, with a sigh of rapture, as she ate a cream date, at the same time twisting her wrist to catch the glitter of her new bangle.

"Yes, but it's 'most half-past eight," said King, "and breakfast's at nine. I'm going to skittle!"

He gathered up his new belongings, and with a sort of combination war-whoop and "Merry Christmas," he scampered away to his room. The two girls followed his example, and soon were busily dressing themselves and helping each other.

Marjorie put on a scarlet cashmere, which, with the big red bows on her hair, made her look very Christmassy, the effect being added to by holly sprigs pinned on here and there. Kitty's frock was a sort of electric blue, that suited her fair hair, and she, too, was holly-decked.

Then, after a hasty inspection of each other, to see that they were all right, the girls skipped downstairs.

So expeditious had they been that not a Maynard was ahead of them, except their father, who had just come down.

"Merry Christmas, girlies!" he cried, and just then everybody came down, almost all at once, and the greetings flew about, as thick as a snowstorm. Grandma Sherwood, in her soft grey breakfast-gown, beamed happily at her brood of grandchildren, and soon they all gathered round the table.

"I wish Christmas was seventy-two hours long, said Marjorie, whose candies had not taken away her appetite for the specially fine breakfast that was being served in honor of the day.

"But you'd fall asleep after twelve hours of it," said Uncle Steve; "so what good would it do you?"

"I wouldn't!" declared King. "I could spend twelve hours having our regular Christmas in the house; and then twelve more outdoors, skating or something; and then twelve more--"

"Eating," suggested his father, glancing at King's plate. "Well, since we can't have seventy-two hours of it, we must cram all the fun we can into twelve. Who's for a run out of doors before we have our Christmas tree?" The three older children agreed to this, and with Mr. Maynard and Uncle Steve they went out for a brisk walk.

"Wish we could snowball," said King, as they returned, and stood for a few moments on the verandah. "It's cold enough, but there no sign of snow."

"Pooh, you don't have to have snow to play a game of snowballs!" said his father. "Why didn't you say what you wanted sooner? You are such a diffident boy! Wait a minute."

Mr. Maynard disappeared into the house, and returned with a large paper bag filled with something, they did not know what.

"Come out on the lawn," he said, and soon they were all out on the brown, dry, winter grass.

"Catch!" and then Mr. Maynard threw to one and another, some swift, white balls. They were really white pop-corn balls, but at first they looked like snow-balls.

The children caught on at once, and soon two or three dozen balls were whiz-zing from each to each, and they had the jolliest game! The balls were too light to hurt if they hit them, yet solid enough to throw well.

To be sure, they broke to bits after many tosses, but the game lasted a half hour, and then Mr. Maynard declared that it was tree time.

"Sounds like tea-time," said Kitty, as they trooped in.

"Sounds a whole lot better than that!" said King.

The tree was in the living-room. It had been brought in, and trimmed after the children went to bed the night before. So they had had no glimpse of it, and were now more than eager to see its glories.

"Are we all here?" asked Mr. Maynard, as he looked over the group in the hall, awaiting the opening of the doors.

"All but Uncle Steve," said Marjorie. "Why doesn't he come?"

"We won't wait for him," said Mr. Maynard, and he gave a loud knock on the double doors of the living-room.

Like magic the doors flew open, and waiting to receive them was Santa Claus himself!

His jolly, smiling face was very red-cheeked, and his white hair and beard streamed down over his red coat, which was of that belted round-about shape that seems to be Santa Claus's. favorite fashion.

His red coat and trousers were trimmed with white fur and gold braid, and his high boots were covered with splashes of white that *looked* like snow. He wore a fur trimmed red cap, and big gold-rimmed spectacles. The latter, with the very red cheeks and long white beard, so changed Uncle Steve's appearance that at first no one seemed to recognize him.

But they knew in a moment, and Marjorie grasped one hand and Kitty the other, as they cried out:

"Hello, Uncle Santa Claus! how did you get so snowy?"

"I came down from the arctic regions, my dears," said the smiling saint, "and up there we have perpetual snow."

"It seems to be perpetual on your boots," observed King; "I'm sure it won't melt off at all!"

"Yes, it's first-class snow," agreed Santa Claus, looking at his boots, which were really splashed with white-wash. "And here's little Miss Rosy Posy," he continued, picking up the baby, who, at first, was a little shy of the strange-looking figure. "This is the very little girl I've come to see, and she must pick something off the tree!"

Rosy Posy recognized Uncle Steve's voice now, and contentedly nestled in his arms as he carried her to the tree. And such a tree as it was!

It reached to the ceiling, and its top boughs had been cut off to get it in the room at all.

The blinds had been closed, and the shades drawn, in order that the illuminations of the tree might shine out brightly, and the gorgeous sight quite took the children's breath away.

The big tree was in the end of the room, and not only did sparkling tinsel rope deck the green branches, but its strands also reached out to the wall on either side, so that the tree seemed to be caught in an immense silver spider-web. Sparkling ornaments decked every limb and twig, and shining among them were hundreds of tiny electric lights of different colors.

Many beautiful presents hung on the tree, without wrappings of any sort to hide their pretty effect, and many more gifts, tied in be-ribboned papers, lay on the floor beneath.

Altogether, it looked as if the whole end of the room were a sort of glittering fairyland, and the children promptly agreed it was the most beautiful tree they had ever had.

As Santa Claus held Baby Rosamond up to select for herself a gift from the tree, he held her so that she faced a big doll, almost as large as herself.

"Oh, that will be my dollie!" she announced, holding out her little arms.

The big doll was detached from its perch and handed to the child, who ran to nurse with her treasure, and would not be parted from it all day long.

Then said Santa Claus: "Marjorie, next, may come and choose anything she would like to use."

He offered his arm, and, with exaggerated ceremony, led Midget to the tree.

She was a little bewildered by the glitter, and the variety of gifts hanging about, but she spied a lovely muff and boa of fluffy white fur that she felt sure must be meant for her.

At any rate they were her choice, and Santa Claus gave them to her with hearty assurance that she had chosen well.

Then he announced: "Next, of course, is little Kitty. Choose, my dear! Take something pretty!"

Kitty advanced slowly. She knew well what she wanted, but she didn't see it on or under the tree.

Santa Claus watched her roving eyes and then said: "If you don't like what you see, look around behind the tree!"

So Kitty peered around, and sure enough, almost hidden by the strands of tinsel, there stood a bookcase.

"I'll choose that!" she cried, in glee, and Mr. Maynard and Santa Claus pulled it out into view. It was the adjustable kind, with glass fronts, and Kitty had long desired just such a one for her room.

"Isn't it beautiful!" she exclaimed, sitting down on the floor to examine it, and to imagine how it would look filled with story books.

"Now, Sir Kingdon, approach," called out Santa Claus; "carefully scan the branches o'er, and help yourself from its ample store!"

King came toward the tree, eying it carefully in search of something he wanted very much, yet scarcely dared hope for.

But, half hidden by a paper fairy, he spied a gleam of gold, and pounced upon the dream of his heart, a gold watch!

"This will do me!" he said, beaming with delight, at the fine time-piece, with its neat fob. It was a handsome affair for a boy of fourteen; but King was careful of his belongings, and Mr. Maynard had decided he could be trusted with it.

Then the elder people received gifts from each other and from the children, and then everybody began to open bundles, and "thank you's" flew around like snowflakes, and tissue paper and gay ribbons were knee deep all over the floor.

"I didn't know there were so many presents in the world!" said Marjorie, who sat blissfully on an ottoman, with her lap full of lovely things, and more on the floor beside her. Grandma had brought her an unset pearl. This was not a surprise, for Grandma had given her a pearl every Christmas of her life, and when the time came for her to wear them, they were to be made into a necklace.

Uncle Steve had brought her a bureau set of ivory, with her monogram on the brushes, and the children gave her various trinkets.

Then Stella and Molly had sent gifts to her, and Gladys and some of the other school girls had also sent Christmas remembrances, with the result that Midget was fairly bewildered at her possessions. The others too, had quantities of things, and Uncle Steve declared that he really had spilled his whole sack at this house, and he must rescue some of the things to take to other children. But he didn't really do this, and the Maynards, as was their custom, arranged their gifts on separate tables, and spent the morning admiring and discussing them.

At two o'clock they had the Christmas feast.

Nurse Nannie played a gay march on the piano, and Mr. Maynard, offering his arm to Grandma, led the way to the dining-room. King, escorting Rosy Posy, walked next, followed by Midget and Kitty. Last of all came Mrs. Maynard and Uncle Steve.

The dining-table was almost as beautiful as the Christmas tree. Indeed, in the centre of it was a small tree, filled with tiny, but exquisite decorations, and sparkling with electric lights. The windows had been darkened, and the shining tree blazed brilliantly.

The table was decorated with red ribbons and holly and red candles, and red candle shades and everybody had red favours and red paper bells.

"I feel like a Robin Redbreast," said Marjorie; "isn't it all beautiful! Did you do it, Mother?"

"Yes, with Sarah's help," said Mrs. Maynard, for her faithful and clever little waitress was of great assistance in such matters.

"It's like eating in an enchanted palace," said Kitty. "Everything is so bright and sparkly and gleaming; and, oh! I'm *so* hungry!"

"Me, too!" chimed in the other young Maynards, and then they proceeded to do ample justice to the good things Ellen sent in in abundance.

But at last even the young appetites were satisfied, and while the elders sipped their coffee in the library, the children were sent off to play by themselves.

The baby was turned over to Nurse Nannie, and the other three tumbled into their wraps and ran out of doors to play off some of their exuberant enthusiasm.

CHAPTER IV
HAPPY NEW YEAR!

I t's been a gay old week, hasn't it?" said Marjorie, on New Year's Eve.

"You bet!" cried King, who sometimes lapsed from the most approved diction. "Wish it was just beginning. We had fine skating till the snow came, and ever since, it's been bang-up sleighing. Well, only four more days, and then school, school, school!"

"Don't remind me of it!" said Marjorie with a groan. "I wish I was a Fiji or whatever doesn't have to go to school at all!"

"Oh, pshaw, Midge; it isn't so bad after you get started. Only holidays make you so jolly that it's hard to sit down and be quiet."

"It's always hard for me to sit down and be quiet," said Midge. "If they'd let me walk around, or sit on the tables or window-sills, I wouldn't mind school so much. It's being cramped into those old desks that I hate."

Poor little Marjorie, so active and restless, it was hard for her to endure the confinement of the schoolroom.

"Why don't you ask mother to let you go to boarding-school, Mops?" asked Kitty, with an air of having suggested a brilliant solution of her sister's difficulties.

Marjorie laughed. "No, thank you, Kitsie," she said. "What good would that do? In the school hours I s'pose I'd have to sit as still as I do here, and out of school hours I'd die of homesickness. Imagine being away off alone, without all of you!"

Kitty couldn't imagine anything like that, so she gave it up.

"Then I guess you'll have to go to school, same's you always have done."

"I guess I will," said Marjorie, sighing. "But there's a few more days' holiday yet, and I'm not going to think about it till I have to. What shall we do to-night? It's the last night of the old year, you know."

"I wonder if they'd let us sit up and see it out," said King.

"We never have," returned Marjorie; "I don't believe Mother'd say yes, though maybe Father would."

"If he does, Mother'll have to," said Kitty, with a knowledge born of experience. "Let's ask 'em."

"It's almost bed-time now," said King, glancing at the clock; "but I'm not a bit sleepy."

The others declared they were not, either, and they all went in search of their parents. They found them in the library, with Uncle Steve and Grandma, who were still visiting them.

"Sit the old year out!" exclaimed Mr. Maynard, when he heard their request. "Why, you're almost asleep now!"

"Oh, we're not a bit sleepy!" protested Marjorie. "Do, Daddy, dear, let us try it,--we never have, you know."

"Why, I've no objections, if Mother hasn't."

Mrs. Maynard looked as if she didn't think much of the plan, but Uncle Steve broke in, saying:

"Oh, let them, of course! It can't do them any harm except to make them sleepy to-morrow, and they can nap all day if they like."

"Yes, let them do it," said Grandma, who was an indulgent old lady. "But I'm glad I don't have to sit up with them."

"I too," agreed Mr. Maynard. "I used to think it was fun, but I've seen so many New Years come sneaking in, that it's become an old, old story."

"That's just it, sir," said King, seeing a point of vantage. "We haven't, you know, and we'd like to see just how they come in."

"Well," said his father, "where will you hold this performance? I can't have you prowling all over the house, waking up honest people who are abed and asleep."

"You must take the nursery," said Mrs. Maynard. "I wouldn't let you stay down-stairs alone, but you may stay in the nursery as late as you like. I daresay by ten or half-past, you'll be glad to give it up, and go to your beds."

"Not we," said King. "Thank you, heaps, for letting us do it. We're going to have a fine time. Come on, girls!"

"One minute, King; you're not to make any noise after ten-thirty. Grandma goes to her room then, and the rest of us soon after."

"All right, we won't. It isn't going to be a noisy party, anyhow."

"Then I don't see how it can be a Maynard party," said Uncle Steve, quizzically, but the children had run away.

"Now, we'll just have the time of our lives!" said King, as the three of them reached the nursery.

"Of course we will," agreed Marjorie. "What shall we do?"

"Let's see, it's nine o'clock. We can play anything till half-past ten; after that we can only do quiet things. Let's play Blind Man's Buff."

"All right, you be *it*."

So King was blindfolded, and he soon caught Kitty, who soon caught Midget, and then she caught King again. But it wasn't very much fun, and nobody quite knew why.

"It makes me too tired," said Kitty, throwing herself on the couch, and fanning her hot little face with her handkerchief. "Let's play a sit-down game."

"But we can play those after we have to be quiet," objected King. "Get up, Kit, you'll fall asleep if you lie there."

"No, I won't," said Kitty, opening her eyes very wide, but cuddling to the soft pillow.

"Yes, you will, too! Come on. Let's play 'animals.' That's noisy enough, and you can sit down too."

"Animals" was a card game where they sat round a table, and as occasion required assumed the voices of certain animals.

"All right," said Kitty, jumping up; "I'll be the Laughing Hyena."

"I'll be a Lion," said King, and Marjorie decided to be a Rooster.

Soon the game was in full swing, and as the roar of the lion, the crowing of the rooster, and the strange noise that represented Kitty's idea of the hyena's mirth, floated downstairs, the grown-ups smiled once more at the irrepressible spirits of the young Maynards. But after they had roared and crowed and laughed for what seemed like an interminable time, King looked at his Christmas watch and exclaimed:

"Goodness, girls! it's only half-past nine! I though it was about eleven!"

"So did I," said Marjorie, trying to hide a yawn.

"Oh, I say, Mops, you're sleepy!"

"I am not, either! I just sort of--sort of choked."

"Well, don't do it again. What shall we play now?"

"Let's sing," said Kitty.

So Marjorie banged away on the nursery piano, and they sang everything they could think of.

"I can't play another note," said Midget, at last. "My fingers are perfectly numb. Isn't it nearly twelve?"

"Isn't ten," said King, closing his watch with a snap. "We've only a half-hour more before we've got to be quiet, so let's make the most of it."

"I'm hungry," said Kitty. "Can't we get something to eat?"

"Good idea!" said King. "Let's forage for some things, and bring them up here, but don't eat them until later. After half-past ten, you know."

So they all slipped down to the pantry, and returned with a collection of apples and cookies, which they carefully set aside for a later luncheon.

"Only twenty minutes left of our noisy time," said King, with a suspicious brisk-ness in his tone. "Come on, girls, let's have a racket."

"There's no racket to me!" declared Kitty, throwing herself on the couch; "I feel--quiet."

"Quiet!" exclaimed her brother. "Kit Maynard, if you're sleepy, you can go to bed! You're too young to sit up with Midge and me, anyhow!"

This touched Kitty in a sensitive spot, as he knew it would.

"I'm not!" she cried, indignantly; "I'm as old as you are, so there!"

King didn't contradict this, which would seem to prove them both a bit sleepy.

"You are, Kitty!" said Marjorie, laughing; "you're older than either of us! So you tell us what to do to keep awake!"

It was out! Marjorie had admitted that they were sleepy.

King grinned a little sheepishly. "Pooh," he said, "it'll pass over if we just get interested in something. Let's read aloud to each other."

"That always puts me to sleep," said Kitty, with a fearful and undisguised yawn.

"Kit! if you do that again, we'll put you out! Now, brace up,--or else go to bed!"

Kitty braced up. Indeed, Kitty had special powers in this direction, if she chose to exercise them.

"Pooh, I can brace up better than either of you," she said, confidently; "and here's how I'm going to do it."

She went over to the big nursery washstand, and turning the cold water faucet, ran the bowl full, and then plunged her face and hands in.

"Kit, you're a genius!" cried her brother, in admiration, as she came up, spluttering, and then made another dash. Soon Kitty's face was hidden in the folds of a rough towel, and the others successively followed her lead.

"My! how it freshens you!" said Marjorie, rubbing her rosy cheeks till they glowed. "I'm as wide awake as anything!"

"So'm I," said King. "Kit, I take off my hat to you! Now it's half-past ten. I move we eat our foods, and then we can have a good time playing parcheesi or jackstraws."

They drew up to the nursery table, and endeavored to enjoy the cookies and apples.

"How funny things taste at night," said Kitty. "I'm not hungry, after all."

"You'd better wash your face again," said Marjorie, looking at her sister's drooping eyelids.

"Do something to her," said King, in despair.

So Marjorie tickled Kitty, until she made her laugh, and that roused her a little.

"I won't go to sleep," she said, earnestly; "truly, I won't. I want to see the New Year come. Let's look out the window for it."

Kitty's plans were always good ones.

Drawing the curtains aside the three stood at the window, their arms about each other.

"Isn't it still?" whispered Marjorie, "and look at the moon!"

A yellow, dilapidated-looking, three-quarter sort of a moon was sinking in the west, and the bark branches of the trees stood out blackly in the half-light.

The roads gleamed white, and the shrubbery looked dark, the whole landscape was weird and unlike the sunny scenes they knew so well.

"I s'pose everybody in the house is abed now, but us," said King. He meant it exultantly, but his voice had a tone of awe, that found an echo in the girls' hearts.

"Come away from the window," said Midge; turning back to the brightly lighted room. "Let's think of something nice to do."

"I can think better here," said Kitty, dropping heavily on the couch, her head, by good luck; striking squarely in the middle of the pillow.

"Kit," said her brother,--"Kitty,--you,--you go to bed,--if you--if you can't--"

As King spoke, he came across a big armchair, and quite unintentionally he let himself fall into it. It felt very pleasant, somehow,--so much so, indeed, that he neglected to finish his admonition to Kitty, and she wouldn't have heard it if he had!

Marjorie, by a strange coincidence, also met a most friendly Morris chair, which held out inviting arms. It seemed a pity to refuse such cordiality, so Marjorie sat down in it a minute to do that thinking they had spoken about. What was it they were to think of? Something about the moon? No, that wasn't it. Her new furs? Not quite; school,--Gladys,--cookies?

These thoughts drifted confusedly about Marjorie's brain for a few moments, and then, with a little tired sigh, her curly head dropped back on the Morris chair's velvet cushion, and her eyes closed.

How those three children *did* sleep! The sound, hard sleep that only healthy, romping children know. When Mrs. Maynard softly opened the door a little later, she almost laughed aloud at the picturesque trio.

But stifling her mirth lest she awake them, she called her husband to her side. After a few whispered words, they went away, and returned with down quilts and steamer rugs, which they gently tucked about the vanquished heroes, and then lowering the lights left them asleep at their posts.

For an hour the children slept soundly, and then, at ten minutes before twelve the nursery door was softly opened again.

This time, Mr. and Mrs. Maynard, accompanied by Grandma Sherwood and Uncle Steve, came in, apparently with the intention of staying. Mr. Maynard snapped on the lights, and the grownups smiled as they gazed on the faces of the sleeping children.

"What time is it, Fred?" asked Mrs. Maynard.

"Seven minutes of twelve."

"Waken them, then. There isn't any too much time."

So Mr. Maynard sprung a small "watchman's rattle." It made a pleasant whirr, but he was obliged to hold it near each child's ear before those deep slumbers were disturbed.

"What is it?" said King, who first opened his eyes. "Kitty, you're asleep!"

His last waking thought possessed him as his eye fell on his sleeping sister, he spoke before he realized that he had been asleep himself.

"What's the matter?" he said, seeing all the people standing about, and noticing the rug over himself.

"Nothing's the matter," answered his father, blithely, "only the New Year is hurrying toward us, and we all want to greet it together."

"You bet we do!" cried King, now broad awake, and shaking himself out of his rug as he jumped up.

Mrs. Maynard was rousing Kitty, and sat beside the half-asleep child with her arm round her, while Grandma was treating Marjorie in the same way.

"It seems a shame," began Grandma, but Uncle Steve interrupted:

"A shame to wake them? Not a bit of it! It would be a shame to let them sleep through a chance that they won't get again for a year! Hello! chickabiddies! Hello! Wake up! Fire! Murder! Thieves! Fred, give me that rattle!"

Taking the noisy little toy, Uncle Steve sprang it vigorously, and was rewarded for his efforts by seeing the two girls at last on their feet and smiling broadly,--wide awake now, indeed.

"Five minutes grace," said Mr. Maynard. "Out with your watches, you who have them. The rest look on with somebody else."

Kitty ran to her father's side, and cuddled in his arm, as she looked at his watch. Marjorie saw Uncle Steve's smile inviting her, so she flew across the room to him; and King politely offered his watch to his mother and grandmother, saying the nursery clock would do for him.

Care was taken to have all the time-pieces set exactly alike, and then it was three minutes of midnight, and they waited.

"He'll come in at the window, the New Year will," said Mr. Maynard as he flung the casement wide open. "The old year is going. Bid him good-bye, children, you'll never see him again. Good-bye, old year, good-bye!"

"Good-bye, old year, good-bye!" they all said in concert, and murmured it again, as the last seconds flew steadily by.

"Happy New Year!" shouted Mr. Maynard, as his second-hand reached the mark, but he was no quicker than the others, and all the voices rang out a "Happy New Year" simultaneously.

Then the village clock began to strike twelve, all the bells in the little town began to ring, some firing was heard, and shouts from passers-by in the streets added to the general jubilee.

"Isn't it splendid!" cried Marjorie, as she leaned out of the window. "The moon is gone, but see the bright, bright stars, all twinkling 'Happy New Year' to us!"

"May it indeed be a Happy New Year for you, my dear child," said her father, as he kissed her tenderly.

And then everybody was exchanging kisses and greetings, and good wishes, and Marjorie realized that at last, she had sat up to "see the New Year in."

"But I don't see how we happened to fall asleep," she said, looking puzzled.

"I, either," said King; "I was just bound I wouldn't, and then I did."

"You were bound I shouldn't, too," said Kitty, "but I did!"

"You all did!" said Mr. Maynard. "Such sleeping I never saw!"

"Well, it was lovely of you to wake us up," said Marjorie; "I wouldn't have missed all this for anything."

"All things come to him who waits," said her father, "and you certainly waited very quietly and patiently!"

"And now, skip to bed," said Mrs. Maynard, "and not until three hundred and sixty-five nights are passed, do we have such a performance as this again."

"All right," said the children, "good-night, and Happy New Year!"

"Good-night and Happy New Year!" echoed the grown-ups.

CHAPTER V
A TEARFUL TIME

The New Year was about a week old, and so far, had nobly fulfilled all hopes of happiness.

To be sure, Marjorie had been obliged to begin school again, but as she had the companionship of Gladys Fulton, who dearly loved to go to school, it helped her to bear the trial.

She had been to spend the afternoon with Gladys and was returning home at five o'clock, as was the rule for winter days.

She turned in at her own gate-way, and had there been any one to see her, it might have been noticed that her demeanor and expression were very unlike the usual appearance of gay, laughing Marjorie Maynard.

In fact, she looked the picture of utter despair and dejection. Her head hung down, her steps were slow, and yet she seemed filled with a riot of indignation.

Her face was flushed and her eyes red, and though not exactly crying, great shivering sobs now and then shook her whole body.

Once inside her own home grounds, she quickened her pace a little, and almost ran up the verandah steps and in at the door.

She slammed it behind her, and though, I am sorry to say, this was not an unusual proceeding for Midget, yet she was truly trying to break herself of the habit.

But this time she gave the door a hard, angry slam, and flinging her wraps anywhere, as she went along, she brushed hastily through the various rooms in search of her mother.

But Mrs. Maynard and Kitty had gone out driving, and King wasn't at home, either, so poor Marjorie, her eyes now blinded with surging tears, stumbled on to her own room, and threw herself, sobbing, on her little white bed.

She buried her face in the pillow and gave way to such tumultuous grief that the brass bedstead fairly shook in sympathy.

"I can't bear it!" she murmured, half aloud; "I **can't** bear it! It's a wicked shame! I don't Want to live any more! Oh, I **wish** Mother would come home!"

For nearly half an hour Marjorie cried and cried. Now with big, bursting, heart-rending sobs, and at quieter intervals, with floods of hot tears.

Her little handkerchief became a useless, wet ball, and she dried her eyes, spasmodically, on various parts of the pillow-case.

At last, in one of her paroxysms of woe, she felt a little hand on her cheek, and Rosy Posy's little voice said, sweetly:

"What 'e matter, Middy? Wosy Posy loves 'oo!"

This was a crumb of comfort, and Marjorie drew the baby's cool cheek against her own hot one.

The child scrambled up on the bed, beside her sister, and petted her gently, saying:

"Don't ky, Middy; 'top kyin'."

"Oh, Rosy Posy, I'm so miserable! where is Mother?"

"Muvver dawn yidin'. Wosy take care of 'oo. Want Nannie?"

"No, I don't want Nannie. You stay here, little sister, till Mother comes."

"Ess. Wosy 'tay wiv Middy. Dear Middy."

The loving baby cuddled up to her sister, and smoothed back the tangled curls with her soft little hand, until exhausted Marjorie, quite worn out with her turbulent storm of tears, fell asleep.

And here Mrs. Maynard found them, as, coming in soon, she went in search of her eldest daughter.

"Why, Baby," she said; "what's the matter? Is Marjorie sick?"

"No," said Rosamond, holding up a tiny finger. "She's aseep. She kied and kied, Middy did, an' nen she went seepy-by, all herself."

"Cried!" exclaimed Mrs. Maynard, looking at Midget's swollen, tear-stained face. "What was she crying about?"

"I donno," answered Rosy, "but she feeled awful bad 'bout somefin'."

"I should think she did! You run away to Nurse, darling; you were good Baby to take care of Midget, but, now, run away and leave her to Mother."

Mrs. Maynard brought some cool water and bathed the flushed little face, and then sprinkling some violet water on a handkerchief she laid it lightly across Midget's brow. After a time the child woke, and found her mother sitting beside her.

"Oh, Mother!" she cried; "oh, Mother!"

"What is it, dearie?" said Mrs. Maynard, putting her arms round Marjorie. "Tell Mother, and we'll make it all right, somehow."

She was quite sure Miss Mischief had been up to some prank, which had turned out disastrously. But it must have been a serious one, and perhaps there were grave consequences to be met.

"Oh, Mother, it's the most dreadful thing!" Here Marjorie's sobs broke out afresh, and she really couldn't speak coherently.

"Never mind," said Mrs. Maynard, gently, fearing the excitable child would fly into hysterics. "Never mind it to-night. Tell me about it to-morrow."

"N-no,--I w-want to tell you now,--only,--I c-can't talk. Oh, Mother, what shall I d-do? G-Gladys--"

"Yes, dear; Gladys,--what did she do? Or perhaps you and Gladys--"

Mrs. Maynard now surmised that the two girls were in some mischievous scrape, and she felt positive that Marjorie had been the instigator, as indeed she usually was.

"Oh, Mother, darling," as something in Mrs. Maynard's tone made Marjorie smile a little through her tears, "it isn't *mischief*! It's a thousand times worse than that!"

Middy was quieter now, with the physical calm that always follows a storm of tears.

"It's this; Gladys is going away! Forever! I mean, they're *all* going to move away,--out west, and I'll never see her again!"

Mrs. Maynard realized at once what this meant to Marjorie. The girls were such good friends, and neither of them cared so much for any one else, as for each other. The Fultons lived just across the street, and had always lived there, through both the little girls' lives. It was almost like losing her own brother or sister, for Marjorie and Gladys were as lovingly intimate as two sisters could be.

Also, it seemed a case where no word of comfort or cheer could be spoken.

So Mrs. Maynard gently caressed her troubled child, and said:

"My poor, darling Midget; I'm *so* sorry for you. Are you sure? Tell me all about it."

"Yes, Mother," went on Marjorie, helped already by her mother's loving sympathy; "they just told me this afternoon. I've been over there, you know, and Gladys and Mrs. Fulton told me all about it. Mr. Fulton isn't well, or something, and for his health, they're all going to California, to live there. And they're going right away! The doctor says they must hurry. And, oh, what *shall* I do without Gladys? I love her so!"

"Dear little girl, this is your first trouble; and it has come to you just in the beginning of this happy New Year. I can't tell you how sorry I am for you, and how I long to help you bear it. But there's no way I can help, except by sympathy and love."

"You *do* help, Mother. I thought I'd *die* before you came!"

"Yes, darling, I know my sympathy helps you, but I mean, I can't do anything to lessen your sorrow at losing Gladys."

"No,--and oh, Mother, isn't it awful? Why, I've *always* had Gladys."

"You'll have to play more with Kitty."

"Oh, of course I love Kit, to play with at home, and to be my sister. But Glad is my chum, my intimate friend, and we always sit together in school, and everything like that. Kitty's in another room, and besides, she has Dorothy Adams for her friend. You know the difference between friends and sisters, don't you, Mother?"

"Of course I do, Midget, dear. You and Kitty are two loving little sisters, but I quite understand how you each love your friends of your own age."

"And Kitty can keep Dorothy, but I must lose Gladys," and Marjorie's sobs broke out anew.

"Why, Mopsy Midget Maynard! Why are we having April showers in January?"

Mr. Maynard's cheery voice sounded in Marjorie's doorway, and his wife beckoned him to come in.

"See what you can do for our little girl," she said; "she is trying to bear her first real trouble, and I'm sure, after these first awful hours she's going to be brave about it."

"What is it, Mops?" said her father, taking the seat Mrs. Maynard vacated. "Tell your old father-chum all about it. You know your troubles are mine, too."

"Oh, Father," said Marjorie, brightening a little under the influence of his strong, helpful voice; "Gladys Fulton is going away from Rockwell to live; and I can't have her for my chum any more."

"Yes, I know; I saw Mr. Fulton and he told me. He's pretty ill, Marjorie."

"Yes, I know it; and I'm awful sorry for him, and for them. But I'm sorry for myself too; I don't want Gladys to go away."

"That's so; you will lose your chum, won't you? By jiminy! it *is* hard lines, little girl. How are you going to take it?"

Marjorie stopped crying, and stared at her father.

"How am I going to take it?" she said, in surprise.

"Yes; that's what I asked. Of course, it's a sorrow, and a deep one, and you'll be very lonely without Gladys, and though your mother and I, and all of us, will help you all we can, yet we can't help much. So, it's up to you. Are you going to give way, and mope around, and make yourself even more miserable than need be; or, are you going to be brave, and honestly try to bear this trouble nobly and patiently?"

Marjorie looked straight into her father's eyes, and realized that he was not scolding or lecturing her, he was looking at her with deep, loving sympathy that promised real help.

"I will try to bear it bravely," she said, slowly; "but, Father, that doesn't make it any easier to have Gladys go."

Mr. Maynard smiled at this very human sentiment, and said:

"No, Midget, dear, it doesn't, in one way; but in another way it does. You mustn't think that I don't appreciate fully your sorrow at losing Gladys. But troubles come into every life, and though this is your first, I cannot hope it will be your last. So, if you are to have more of them, you must begin to learn to bear them rightly, and so make them help your character-growth and not hinder it."

"But, Father, you see Gladys helps my character a lot. She loves to go to school, and I hate it. But if I go with her, and sit with her I don't mind it so much. But without her,--oh how *can* I go to school without her?"

Again Marjorie wept as one who could not be comforted, and Mr. Maynard realized it was truly a crisis in the little girl's life.

"Marjorie," he said, very tenderly, "it *is* a hard blow, and I don't wonder it is crushing you. Nor do I expect you to take a philosophical view of it at present. But, my child, we'll look at it practically, at least. Gladys *is* going; nothing can change that fact. Now, for my sake, as well as your own, I'm going to **ask** you to be my own brave daughter, and not disappoint me by showing a lack of cheerful courage to meet misfortune."

"I don't want to be babyish, Father," said Midget, suddenly feeling ashamed of herself.

"You're not babyish, dear; it's right and womanly to feel grief at losing Gladys; but since it has to be, I want you to conquer that grief, and not let it conquer you."

"I'll try," said Midge, wiping away some tears.

"You know, Marjorie, the old rhyme:

"'For every evil under the sun, There is a remedy, or there's none; If there is one, try to find it, And if there is none, never mind it.'

"Now, I don't say 'never mind it' about this matter, but since there's no remedy, do the best you can to rise above it, as you will have to do many times in your future years."

"Father," said Marjorie, thoughtfully; "that sounds awful noble, but I don't believe I quite understand. What can I **do** to 'rise above it'?"

"Marjorie, you're a trump! I'd rather you'd be practical, than wise. And there's no better weapon with which to fight trouble than practicality. Now, I'll tell you what to do. And I don't mean today or tomorrow, for just at first, you wouldn't be a human little girl if you **didn't** nearly cry your eyes out at the loss of your friend. But soon,--say about next Tuesday,--if you could begin to smile a little, and though I know it will be hard, smile a little wider and wider each day--"

"Till the top of my head comes off?" said Marjorie, smiling already.

"Yes; theoretically. But make up your mind that since Gladys must go, you're not going to let the fact turn you into a sad, dolorous mope instead of Mops."

"That's all very well at home, Father dear, but I'll miss her so at school."

"Of course you will; but is there any remedy?"

"No, there isn't. I don't want any other seat-mate, and I don't want to sit alone."

"Oh! Well, I can't see any way out of that, unless I go and sit with you."

Marjorie had to laugh at this. "You couldn't squeeze in the space," she said.

"Well, then you've proved there's *no* remedy. So, never mind it! I mean that, dearie. When you are lonely and just fairly *aching* for Gladys, put it bravely out of your mind."

"How can I?"

"Why, fill your mind with something else that will crowd it out. Say to yourself, 'There's that sorrow poking his head up again, and I must push him down.' Then go at something *hard*. Study your spelling, or go on a picnic, *anything* to crowd that persistent sorrow out."

"Can't I ever think of Gladys?"

"Oh, yes, indeed! but think gay, happy thoughts. If memories of your good times make you sad, then cut them out, and wonder what sort of fun she's having where she is. Write her nice, cheery letters. Letters are lots of fun."

"Indeed they are," said Marjorie, brightening. "I'll love to get her letters."

"Of course you will. And you can send each other postcards and little gifts, and if you try you can have a lot of pleasure with Gladys in spite of old sorrow."

"Daddy, you're such a dear! You've helped me a heap."

"That's what daddys are for, Midget mine. You're one of my four favorite children, and don't you suppose I'd help you to the earth, if you wanted it?"

"I 'spect you would. And, Father, you said I could cry till about Tuesday, didn't you?"

"Why, yes; but make it a little shorter spell each day, and,--if perfectly convenient, arrange to do it when I'm at home."

"Oh, Father, that's the time I won't cry! When you're here to talk to me."

"You don't say so! Then I'll retire from business, close up my office, and stay at home all day hereafter. Anything I can do to help a lady in distress, must be done!"

They were both laughing now, and Midge had quite stopped crying, though her heart was heavy underneath her smiles.

But the whole current of her thoughts had been changed by her talk with her father, and as she made herself tidy, and went down to dinner, she felt a responsibility on her to act as became the brave daughter of such a dear father.

And, strange to say, the feeling was not entirely unpleasant.

CHAPTER VI
THE GOING OF GLADYS

Gladys was to go away early one Saturday morning.

On Friday afternoon Marjorie gave a little farewell party for her. Mrs. Maynard arranged this as a pleasant send-off for Marjorie's friend, and determined that though it was a sad occasion, it should be also a merry one.

So, instead of depending on the guests to make their own entertainment, a professional entertainer had been engaged from New York, and he sang and recited and did pantomimes that were so funny nobody could help laughing.

And, too, though all the children liked Dick and Gladys Fulton, yet none felt so very sorry to have them leave Rockwell as Marjorie did.

Even Kingdon, though he was good chums with Dick, had other chums, and, while sorry to have Dick go, he didn't take it greatly to heart.

Marjorie was truly trying to be brave, but she looked at Gladys with a heart full of love and longing to keep her friend near her.

As for Gladys, herself, she, too, was sad at leaving Marjorie, but she was so full of wonder and curiosity about the new home they were going to, in the land of flowers and sunshine, that she was fairly impatient to get there.

"Just think, Mopsy," she said, as the two girls sat together at the party feast, "the roses out there are as big as cabbages, and bloom all the year round."

"Are they really?" said Midget, interested in spite of herself.

"Yes, and I'll send you a big box of them as soon as I get there. They'll keep all right, 'cause mother received a box the other day, and they were as fresh as fresh."

"And you'll write to me, Glad, won't you?" said Marjorie, a little wistfully.

"'Course I will! I'll write every week, and you write every week. What day do you choose?"

"Monday; that comes first."

"All right. You write to me every Monday, and I'll write to you every Thursday."

"You can't answer a Monday letter on Thursday," put in Gladys's brother Dick; "it takes five or six days for a letter to go."

"Well, I'll write the Monday after you go," said Marjorie, "and then you answer it as soon as you get it; then I'll answer yours as soon as I get it, and so on."

"All right, I will. And I'll write you a letter while I'm on the train, travelling. Of course we'll be five or six days getting there ourselves."

"So you will. Oh, Gladys, California is awful far away!"

"Yes, isn't it! But, Mops, maybe you can come out there and visit me some time."

Marjorie looked doubtful. "No," she said, "I don't think I could go and leave them all, and I don't s'pose you mean for us all to come."

"No, I meant just you. Well, I'll come here and visit you, some time, how's that?"

"Lovely!" cried Midge, with sparkling eyes. "Oh, will you, Gladys? That will be something to look forward to. Will you?"

"Of course I will, Mops, dear. I know mother'll let me, and I'd love to come."

This was a real consolation, and Marjorie laid it up in her heart for comfort on lonely days.

After the party supper was over, most of the young guests gave Gladys or Dick little gifts which they had brought them as remembrances.

They were merely pretty trifles, but the Fulton children were greatly pleased, and declared they should never forget their Rockwell friends for any they might make in California.

Marjorie gave Gladys a gold neck-chain, with a little gold heart containing her picture, and Gladys had already given Midge her own portrait framed in silver to stand on her dressing-table. The young guests all went away except the two Fultons, who were to stay to dinner. Mr. Maynard came home, and with a determination to keep Marjorie's spirits up, he was especially gay and nonsensical.

"I suppose Uncle Sam will have to put on extra mail service when you two girls get to corresponding," he said.

"Yes, Mr. Maynard," said Gladys. "Marjorie and I are both going to write every week, and I'm going to send her flowers by mail."

"Well, don't send any live rattlesnakes or Gila monsters in the mail. They might starve on the way."

"I'd rather they'd starve on the way than reach here alive," said Marjorie, with a little shudder.

"Do they have those things where you're going, Glad?"

"I don't know. Isn't it strange to be going to live in a place that you don't know anything about?"

"It's strange to have you live anywhere but in Rockwell," said Marjorie, and Gladys squeezed her hand under the table.

But at last the time came for the real farewells.

"Cut it short," cried Mr. Maynard, gaily, though there was a lump in his own throat as Gladys and Marjorie threw their arms about each other's neck for the last time.

The Fultons were to leave very early the next morning, and the girls would not meet again.

Both were sobbing, and Dick and Kingdon stood by, truly distressed at their sisters' grief.

"Come, dearie, let Gladys go now," said Mrs. Maynard, for knowing Marjorie's excitable nature, she feared these paroxysms of tears.

"No, no! she shan't go!" Midge almost screamed, and Gladys was also in a state of convulsive weeping.

Mr. Maynard went to Marjorie, and laid his big cool hand on her brow.

"My little girl," he whispered in her ear "father wants you to be brave *now*."

Midget look up into his dear, kind eyes, and then, with a truly brave effort she conquered herself.

"I will, Father," she whispered back, and then, with one last embrace, she said, "Good-bye, Gladys, dear Gladys, good-bye."

She let her go, and Dick took his sister's arm in silence, and they went away.

Both Mr. and Mrs. Maynard were somewhat shaken by the children's tragedy, but neither thought it wise to show it.

"Now, Mopsy Moppet," said her father, "what do you think I have here?"

He took a parcel from the mantel, and held it up.

"I don't know," said Midge, trying to smile; "what is it?"

"Well, it's a game,--a brand new game, and none of your poky old go-to-sleep affairs either. It's a lively, wide-awake game, that only lively, wide-awake children can play. So come one, come all!"

They all gathered round the table, and Mr. Maynard explained the rules of the new game. Marjorie loved games, and as this was really a most interesting one, she couldn't help enjoying it, and was soon absorbed in the play. It combined the elements of both skill and chance, and caused many moments of breathless suspense, as one or another gained or lost in the count.

When it was finished, Marjorie was again her own rosy, smiling self, and though she still felt the vague weight of sorrow, she had spent a pleasant, enjoyable hour.

"And now to bed, chickadees," cried their father, "it's long past nine!"

"Is it really?" exclaimed Midget, "how the time has flown!"

"That's because you were my own brave girl, and tried to rise above misfortune," said Mr. Maynard, as he bade her good-night. "No teary pillows to-night, girlie."

"No, Father, dear, I hope not."

"Just go to sleep, and dream that you have a few friends still east of the Rockies."

"More than I'll ever have west of them," responded Marjorie, and then with her arm round Kitty's waist, the two girls went upstairs to bed.

The next morning at the breakfast table, Mr. Maynard made a sudden and unexpected announcement.

"Mother Maynard," he said, "if you can spare your eldest daughter, I think I'll borrow her for the day."

"What!" cried Marjorie, looking up in surprise.

"You may have her," said Mrs. Maynard, smiling, "if you'll return her safely."

"Oh, I can't promise that. I'm of rather careless habits, and I might mislay her somewhere."

"Well, I'll trust you for this once. Mops, do you want to go to town with Father?"

Marjorie's eyes flashed an answer, and Kitty exclaimed:

"Without us?"

"I grieve to disappoint you, Kitsie," said Mr. Maynard, "but you still have your friend Dorothy. Midget is cruelly deprived of her chum, and so for one day she is going to put up with a doddering old gentleman instead. Get your bonnet and shawl, my child."

Marjorie looked at her mother for confirmation of this good news, and receiving an answering smile, she excused herself from the table and ran away to her room. Nannie helped her, and soon she tripped downstairs prettily dressed in a dark blue cloth frock and jacket, a blue felt hat, and her Christmas furs.

"Whew! what a fine lady!" said her father. "I shall have to don my best hat and feathers, I think."

"I've lost my chum, too," said King, as he watched the pair about to start.

"Yes, you have, my boy, but he wasn't your 'perfectly darling confidential friend,' as girls' chums are! Moreover, you haven't shed such gallons of first-class well-salted tears as this young person has. No, Son, I'm sorry to leave you behind, but you didn't weep and wail loud enough!"

King had to laugh at the way his father put it, but he well knew Marjorie was given a day's pleasure to divert her mind from Gladys's departure, and he didn't begrudge his sister the trip.

"We must be extra kind to old Midge, Kit," he said, as Marjorie and her father walked briskly down the drive.

"Yes," said Kitty, earnestly, "she does feel awful about losing Gladys. I'm going to make fudge for her, while she's gone to-day."

"I wish I could do something for her. Boys are no good!"

"You are too!" cried loyal little Kitty. "You can help her with her arithmetic every night. She can do it all right, if she has a little help, and Glad used to help her a lot."

"Good for you, Kitsie! of course I will. Dear old Midge, I'm terrible sorry for her."

Meantime, Marjorie, by her father's side, was rushing along in the train to New York.

While Mr. Maynard read his paper, he glanced sometimes at his daughter, and rejoiced that she was interestedly gazing out of the window at the flying scenery.

Occasionally, she turned and smiled at him, but she said little, and he knew she was being brave and trying not to think too much about her loss.

Gladys had gone away early and when they had passed the closed and deserted-looking Fulton house, Marjorie had swallowed hard and looked the other way.

But once in New York, the child had no time to think of anything but the present hour, so full of joy was the whole day.

"My time is yours," announced Mr. Maynard, as they reached the city. "I've telephoned to the office that I won't be there at all today, so what shall we do?"

"Oh, Father, a whole Ourday, all for you and me?" Marjorie's eyes danced at this unheard of experience.

"Yes, Midget; partly because I'm sorry for my troubled little girl, and partly because you *are* bearing your trouble bravely and cheerfully."

"Who wouldn't be cheerful, with a whole Ourday, and a whole father, all to myself!"

"Well, you'll probably never have another, alone with me. So make the most of it. Where shall we go first?"

"Oh, I don't know; it's all so lovely."

"Then I'll choose. Step this way, Madame."

This way, was toward a line of waiting taxicabs, and Mr. Maynard engaged one, and handed Marjorie in.

"A taxy ride! Oh, lovely!" she cried, as they started off at a fine pace.

On they went, spinning across town, till they reached Fifth Avenue, and turned up that broad thoroughfare.

Marjorie enjoyed every minute, and looked out of the open window at the bustling city life all about. Up town they went for blocks and blocks, and stopped at the Metropolitan Art Museum.

They went in here, after Mr. Maynard had dismissed the cab, and staid the rest of the morning.

Marjorie, perhaps, would not have cared so much for the pictures and statues had she been alone; but her father called her attention to certain ones, and told her about them in such a way, that she was amused and instructed both.

They looked at strange and curious relics of ancient times; they studied the small models of the world's greatest buildings; and they lingered in the hall full of casts of the noblest statues of all time.

"Hungry, Chickadee?" said Mr. Maynard, at last, looking at his watch.

"Why, yes, I believe I am; but I hadn't thought of it."

"I'm glad you are, for I can assure you I am. Suppose we make a mad dash for a pie-shop."

"Come on," said Marjorie, and away they went, through the turnstiles, and out upon Fifth Avenue again.

Mr. Maynard hailed a motor-omnibus, and Marjorie carefully climbed the spiral staircase at the back. Her father followed, and sitting up on top of the 'bus, in the crisp, wintry air and bright sunshine, they went whizzing down the avenue.

"Isn't it fun, Father!" said Marjorie, as she held tightly to his arm.

"Yes, and there's a fine view to-day." He pointed out many famous buildings, and when they neared a large hotel, he said:

"We'll have to get out, Midge. I shall pine away with hunger before another block."

"Out we go!" was the reply, and they clambered down the twisty stair.

"Is there anything that would tempt your appetite, Miss Maynard?" said her father, as, seated at a small round table, he looked over the menu.

"No, thank you; I don't think I can eat a thing!" said Midge, dropping her eyes, and trying to look fragile and delicate.

"No? But really, you must try to taste of something. Say, the left wing of a butterfly, with hard sauce."

This made Marjorie laugh, and she said, "I couldn't eat it all, but I might nibble at it."

Then what Mr. Maynard really did, was to order Marjorie's favourite dishes.

First, they had grape-fruit, all cut in bits, and piled up in dainty, long-stemmed glasses. Then, they had a soft, thick soup, and then sweetbreads with mushrooms.

"You're not to get ill, you know," said Mr. Maynard, as Marjorie showed a surprising appetite, "but I do want you to have whatever you like to-day."

"Oh, I won't get ill," declared Marjorie, gaily, "and now, may I select the ice cream?"

"Yes, if you won't ask for plum pudding also."

"No, but I do want little cakes, iced all over. Pink and green and white and yellow ones."

These were allowed, and Marjorie blissfully kept on nibbling them, while Mr. Maynard sipped his coffee. In the afternoon they went to a matinee. It was one of the gorgeous spectacular productions, founded upon an old fairy tale, and Marjorie was enraptured with the beautiful tableaux, the wonderful scenery, and the gay music.

"Oh, Father," she said, "aren't we having the gorgeousest time! You are the beautifulest man in the whole world!"

After the performance, Mr. Maynard spoke of going home, but Marjorie's eyes held a mute appeal, which he could not resist.

"Ice cream *again!*" he said, though she had not spoken the words. "Well, ice cream it is, then, but no rich cakes this time. I promised Motherdy I'd bring you home safe and sound. But I'll tell you, we'll buy some of those cakes to take home, and you may have them to-morrow."

"And Kitty and King, too," said Midge. "And let's take them some buttercups."

So the candy and cakes were bought and carried home by two tired but very happy people, and Marjorie fully appreciated the lovely day her father had given her, because of Gladys's going away.

"And I *will* be good and brave," she resolved to herself, on her way home in the train. "I'm going to try to be just as cheerful and pleasant as If Gladys hadn't gone away at all, but was in her own house, across the street."

CHAPTER VII
THE COMING OF DELIGHT

But though Marjorie made her brave resolutions in good faith, it was hard to keep them. School was awful. The very sight of Gladys's empty seat made Midge choke with tears.

Miss Lawrence appreciated the case, and was most gentle and kind to Marjorie, but still the trouble was there.

"Wouldn't you like to have Katy Black sit with you, dear?" asked the teacher.

"No, thank you." said Midge, "I can't bear to put any one in Gladys's place. Don't bother about me, Miss Lawrence, I'm not going to cry."

She didn't cry, but she sighed so frequently and so deeply, that kind-hearted Miss Lawrence almost wept in sympathy.

At home it was better. The Maynards always had good times at home, and of course when there, Marjorie didn't miss Gladys so much. But the long mornings in the school-room, and the long afternoons when she wanted to run over to Gladys's house were almost unbearable.

Merry, madcap Midget became a sober-faced little girl, who was all the more pathetic because she tried to be cheerful.

Mrs. Maynard felt worried about the matter, and proposed to her husband that she should take Marjorie, and go away for a trip somewhere.

"No," said Mr. Maynard; "let her fight it out. It's hard for her, but it's doing her real good, and bringing out the best side of her nature. We'll all help her all we can, and if I'm not greatly mistaken our Marjorie will come out of this ordeal with flying colors."

"It's will-power, little daughter," said Mr. Maynard to her one evening. "Just determine that this cloud shall not entirely obscure the sun for you."

"Yes," said Midge, smiling, "it's just an eclipse, isn't it?"

"Yes, and it seems to be a total eclipse; but even total eclipses pass, if we wait long enough. Any letter from Gladys this week?"

"One came this morning. Would you like to read it?"

"Of course I should, very much."

"It's strange," said Marjorie, as she produced the letter, "for all Gladys loves school so, and is a good student, she can't seem to spell right."

"I know another lady who has difficulty in that direction," said Mr. Maynard, smiling.

"Yes, but Glad is different. She can spell the spelling-book stickers, 'embarrassed,' and 'cleemosynary,' and such words, 'cause she studies them; and then she'll misspell simple every-day words. Now, you see."

Mr. Maynard smiled a little as he read the letter.

Los Angeles, Cal.

DEAR MARJORIE:

We are having a lovely time. We have not found a house yet, but are staying at the hotel till we do find one to suite us, I like it here very much. I miss you very much, dear Marjorie. There are lovely people in the hotel, and we go for walks to pick flowers. The flowers here are beautiful. Now I must close. With lots of love and kisses, your

LOVING GLADYS.

"Between you and me and the post, Midget, I don't think that's a very interesting letter, do you?"

"No, Father, I don't. I thought Glad would write more as she talks. She doesn't talk a bit like that, when we're together."

"I know it, Mops, I've heard her. But some people never can write as they talk. As soon as they get a pen between their fingers, their brain seems to freeze up, and break off in little, cold, hard sentences. Now, what sort of a letter do you write?"

"Here's the answer I wrote to-day to Gladys. I haven't sent it yet."

MY DARLING GLADYS:

I wish you would come back. It's perfectly horrid at school without you, and though Miss Lawrence said Katy Black could sit with me, I don't want her. She's a nice enough girl, but she isn't you. And nobody is, Dear old Glad, I do miss you so.

Of course as there's no remedy under the sun, I'm being cheerful and gay about it, but my heart misses you just the same. We don't have the Jinks Club any more. It made me sick to go to it without you. I expect you're having good times in California, and I'm glad of that. Write soon to

YOUR LOVING MOPSY MIDGET.

"Now, of the two, Midge, yours is the much better letter. Don't ever try to copy Gladys's style, will you?"

"No; I'm glad you like mine best. You see, I write without thinking about anything except not to spill the ink."

"A very good plan. Stick to it all your life. Midget, I don't want to be unkind, but has it struck you that Gladys is not so heart-broken over your separation as you are?"

A look of pain came into Marjorie's loyal eyes, as she said:

"It does seem so, I know. But I think it's because Gladys has all sorts of new places and new people to amuse her, while I'm left here alone."

"It's partly that, little girl; and partly because Gladys hasn't such a warm, loving loyal heart as my Marjorie's."

"She is different," admitted Midget; "but I know she loves me, even if it doesn't say so right out in her letter."

"Perhaps she forgot to put it in, because she was so busy trying not to spill the ink."

"Perhaps so," agreed Marjorie, answering the twinkle in her father's eye.

"And now, Miss Mops, I have a bit of news for you. The Fulton house is rented to some people from New York."

"Is it?" said Marjorie, indifferently.

"And in the family is a girl twelve years of age."

"And you think she'll take Glad's place!" cried Midge, indignantly. "Well, I can just tell you she won't! A girl from New York! She'll be stuck-up, and superior, and look down on us Rockwell girls!"

"How do you know all this?"

"I know; 'cause Katy Black had a girl from New York visiting her, and she was just horrid! All stiff and mincy, and dropping curtseys every two minutes!"

"But you're taught to drop curtseys."

"Yes, when I enter or leave a room where there are ladies, but that girl was always at it, in school and everywhere."

"Sort of a jumping-jack, wasn't she? Well, try to like this new girl, dearie; it's the best I can do for you in the way of neighbors."

"Oh, I may like her,--and I'll be polite to her, of course; but I know I shan't want her for an intimate friend, like Glad."

"Perhaps not; but I was so pleased when I heard a little girl was coming to live across the street, that I think you ought to be pleased too."

"Well, I will! I am! And if she isn't too stuck-up, I'll try to like her."

A few afternoons later, King, who was sitting by a front window, called out:

"Hi! I say, Mops! Here's the new family moving into the Fulton house!"

Marjorie only upset a waste-basket and a very small table as she ran to the window to look out.

Kitty raced after her, and Rosy Posy toddled up too, so in a moment the four were eagerly gazing at the new-comers, themselves quite hidden by the lace curtains.

"Nice looking bunch," commented King, as he watched a well-dressed lady and gentleman get out of the carriage.

"And there's the girl!" cried Marjorie, as a child followed them. "Oh, she *is* a stuck-up!"

"How do you know?" said King. "I think she's a daisy!"

They could only see her back, as the new neighbor walked up the path to the house, but she seemed to be of a dainty, not to say finicky type.

She wore a large hat with feathers, and a black velvet coat that covered her frock completely.

A mass of fluffy golden hair hung below the big black hat, and the little girl tripped along in a way that if not "mincing," was certainly "citified."

"No, I don't like her," declared Midge, as she watched the stranger go up the steps and into the house; "she isn't a bit like Gladys."

"Neither am I," said King, "but you like me."

"Yes, you dear, cunning little sweet thing, I do like you," said Midget, touching King's hair in a teasing way.

He promptly pulled off her hair-ribbon, and as Marjorie felt in the humor, this began one of their favorite games of make-believe.

"The diamond tiara!" she shrieked, "the villain hath stole it!"

"Horrors!" cried Kitty, "then shall he be captured, and forced to restore it!"

She pounced on King, and aided by Marjorie, they threw him on the couch, and wrapped his head in the afghan. Horrible growls came from the prisoner, but no word of surrender.

"Art vanquished?" asked Kitty pulling the afghan away from one of his eyes.

"I art not!" he declared in a muffled voice, but with so terrific a glare from that one eye, that they hastily covered him up again.

But he managed to free himself, and stood towering above the terror-stricken girls, who now knelt at his feet and begged for mercy.

"Spare us!" moaned Kit. "We are but lorn damsels who seek food and shelter!"

"Me wants a selter, too," announced Rosy Posy, joining the others, and clasping her little fat hands as they did. "What is a selter?"

"A selter for none of you!" roared King, with threatening gestures. "To the dungeon, all three! Ha, varlets, appear, and do my bidding!"

"I'll be a varlet," said Midge, suddenly changing her role. "We'll put Lady Katherine in the dungeon, and let the fair Lady Rosamond go free!"

"As thou sayest," said King, agreeably, and, though bravely resisting, Kitty was overpowered, and thrown into a dungeon under the table. From this she contrived to escape by the clever expedient of creeping out at the other side, but as it was then time to get ready for dinner, the game came to an untimely end.

"We've seen the new girl, Father," said Marjorie, as they sat at the table.

"Have you? Well, I've seen the new man,--that is, if you refer to our new neighbors across the street."

"Yes, in Gladys's house. What's his name, Father?"

"Mr. Spencer. I met him at the post-office, and Mr. Gage introduced us. Mr. Gage is the agent who has the Fulton house in charge, and he told we before that these newcomers are fine people. I liked Mr. Spencer exceedingly. I'm sorry, Mops, you're so determined not to like the daughter. Mr. Spencer tells me she's a lovable child."

"Oh, of course he'd think so,--he's her father."

"Well, I admit, fathers are a prejudiced class. Perhaps I have too high an opinion of my own brood."

"You couldn't have," said Kitty, calmly, and Mr. Maynard laughed as he looked at the four smiling faces, and responded:

"I don't believe I could!"

"Don't spoil them, Fred," said Mrs. Maynard, warningly, but King broke in:

"Too late, Mother! We're spoiled already. Father's high opinion of us has made us puffed up and conceited."

"Nonsense, King," cried Midge; "we're not conceited. Not nearly as much so as that girl across the way. You ought to see, Father, how she hopped up the walk! Like a scornful grasshopper!"

"Marjorie," said Mrs. Maynard, repressing a smile, "you must not criticise people so; especially those you don't know."

"Well, she did, Mother. She thinks because she came from New York, Rockwell people are no good at all."

"How do you know that, Midge?" said her father, a little gravely.

"Oh, Midget is a reader of character," said King. "She only saw this girl's yellow hair, hanging down her back, and she knew all about her at once."

"She had a velvet coat," protested Marjorie, "and a short dress and long black legs--"

"You wouldn't want her to wear a train, would you?" put in Kitty.

"No, but her frock was awful short, and her hat was piled with feathers."

"That will do, Marjorie," said her father, very decidedly, now. "It isn't nice to run on like that about some one you've never met."

"But I'm just telling what I saw, Father."

"But not in a kind spirit, my child. You're trying to make the little girl appear unattractive, or even ridiculous; and you must not do that. It isn't kind."

"That's so," said Marjorie, contritely; "it's horrid of me, I know, and I'll stop it. But she did look like a flyaway jib!"

"What is a flyaway jib?" said her father, with an air of one seeking information.

"I haven't an idea," said Mops, laughing; "but I know I've heard of it somewhere."

"And so you describe a girl whom you don't know, in words whose meaning you don't know! Well, that's consistent, at any rate! Now, I *do* know something about this young lady. And, to begin with, I know her name."

"Oh, what is it?" said Midge and Kitty together.

"Well, Mops is such a reader of character, she ought to be able to guess her name. What do you think it is, Midget?"

Marjorie considered. She dearly loved to guess, even when she had no hint to go by.

"I think," she said, slowly, "it is probably Arabella or Araminta."

"'Way off," said her father; "you're no good at guessing. Kitty, what do you say?"

"It ought to be Seraphina," said Kitty, promptly. "She looks like a wax doll."

"Wrong again! King, want to guess?"

"'Course I do. I think her name is Flossy Flouncy. She looks so dressy and gay."

"That's a good name, King," said Marjorie, "and just suits her. I shall call her that, what ever her real name is. I suppose it's Mary Jane, or something not a bit like her. What is it, Father?"

"Well, it's not a common name, exactly. It's Delight."

"Delight!" cried King. "What a funny, name! I never heard of it before."

"I think it's lovely," declared Marjorie. "It's a beautiful name. Why didn't you name me Delight, Mother?"

"You didn't say you wanted me to," returned Mrs. Maynard, smiling, for Marjorie often wished for various names that pleased her better than her own for the moment.

"Well, I think it's sweet, don't you, Kit?"

"Beautiful!" said Kitty, enthusiastically.

"And she's not at all 'stuck-up,'" went on Mr. Maynard; "she's rather shy, and though she wants to get acquainted with you children, she's afraid you won't like her. I didn't tell Mr. Spencer that you had decided already not to like her."

"I like her name," said Marjorie, "but I don't like her because she lives in Gladys's house, and she isn't Gladys!"

"So that's where the shoe pinches!" said Mr. Maynard, laughing at Marjorie's troubled face. "A foolish resentment because strangers are in your friend's home.

Why, dearie, Mr. Fulton was most anxious to rent the house, and he'll be glad to have such good tenants. And, by the way, Midge, don't say anything more unpleasant about the little Spencer girl. You've said enough."

"I won't, Father," said Midget, with an honest glance from her big, dark eyes into his own, for truth to tell, she felt a little ashamed of her foolish criticisms already.

"Delight!" she said, musingly as she and Kitty were preparing for bed that night. "Isn't it a dear name, Kit? What does it make you think of?"

"A princess," said Kitty, whose imagination Was always in fine working order; "one who always wears light blue velvet robes, and eats off of gold dishes."

"Yes," agreed Marjorie, falling in with the game, "and she has white doves fluttering about, and black slaves to bow before her."

"No, not black slaves; they're for princesses named Ermengarde or Fantasmagoria." Kitty was not always particular about any authority for names, if they sounded well. "A princess named Delight would have handmaidens,--fair-haired ones, with soft trailing white robes."

"Kit, you're a wonder," said Marjorie, staring at her younger sister; "how do you know such things?"

"They come to me," said Kitty, mystically.

"Well, they sound all right, but I don't believe handmaidens ought to wear trailing gowns. How could they handmaid?"

"That's so," said Kitty, a little crestfallen.

"Never mind; I spect they could. They could gracefully throw the trails over their arms, as they glide along in their sandalled feet."

"Yes, and strains of music came from concealed luters--"

"Huh! looters are burglars, and it's slang besides."

"No, not that kind. Luters that play on lutes, I mean. And the Princess Delight would sniff attar of rose, and fan herself with waving peacock feathers."

"A slave ought to do that."

"Well, all right, let him. And then the Princess falls asleep 'neath her silken coverlet, and lets her sister put out the lights,--like this!" and with a jump, Kitty bounced into her own little bed, and pulled up the down coverlet to her chin.

Imitating the white-robed handmaidens, Marjorie swayed around to an improvised chant of her own, and putting out the electric lights with much dramatic elaboration, she finally swayed into her own bed, and after they had both chanted a choric good-night, they soon fell sleep.

CHAPTER VIII
A VISIT TO CINDERELLA

One afternoon Marjorie sat by the fire reading. She was not specially interested in her book, but Kitty had gone to see Dorothy Adams, and King was off somewhere, so she had no one to play with.

Presently Sarah entered.

"There's somebody wants you on the telephone, Miss Marjorie," she said, and Midget jumped up, wondering who it could be.

"Hello," she said, as she took the receiver.

"Hello," said a pleasant voice; "is this Marjorie Maynard?"

"Yes; who is this?"

"This is Cinderella."

"Who!"

"Cinderella. My two stepsisters have gone to a ball, and my cruel stepmother has beaten me and starved me--"

"What are you talking about? Who is this, please?"

"Me. I'm Cinderella. And I'm so lonely and sad I thought perhaps you'd come over to see me."

A light began to dawn on Marjorie.

"Oh," she continued, "where do you live?"

"Across the street from your house."

"Then you're Delight Spencer."

"Yes, I am. Can't you come over and let's get acquainted?"

"Yes, I will. I'd like to. Shall I come now?"

"Yes, right away. Good-bye."

"Good-bye."

Marjorie hung up the receiver and after a hasty brush at her curls, and a few pinches at her hair ribbons, she flung on hat and coat and flew across the street.

If only this new girl should be a desirable chum!

That opening about Cinderella sounded hopeful,--she must know how to play.

Well, at any rate, Midget would soon know now.

She rang the bell at Gladys's house, with a queer feeling, and as she went in, and saw the familiar rooms and furniture, and no Gladys, she almost started to run away again--

"Miss Delight wants you to come right up to her room, Miss," said the maid who admitted her, and Marjorie followed her upstairs, glad to find that at least the new girl didn't have Gladys's room for her own. The maid indicated the room, and stood aside for Marjorie to enter, but at the first glance Midget stood still on the threshold.

In the first place the room was transformed. It had been the Fultons' playroom, and furnished rather plainly; but now it was so full of all sorts of things, that it looked like a bazaar.

In a big armchair sat Delight. She had on a Japanese quilted kimona of light blue silk, and little blue Turkish slippers. Her hair was pure golden, and was just a tangle of fluffy curls topped by a huge blue bow.

But her face, Marjorie thought at once, was the most beautiful face she had ever seen. Big blue eyes, a soft pink and white complexion, and red lips smiling over little white teeth, made Delight look like the pictures on Marjorie's fairy calendar.

And yet, as Midget stood for a moment, looking at her, the pink faded from her cheeks, and she rose from her chair, and said, stiffly:

"Sit down, won't you? I'm glad you came."

Marjorie sat down, on the edge of a couch, and Delight sank back in her big chair.

She was so evidently overcome with a spasm of shyness that Midget was sorry for her, but somehow it made her feel shy, herself, and the two little girls sat there, looking at each other, without saying a word.

At last, overcoming her embarrassment, Marjorie said, "Was it you who telephoned?" A sudden wave of red flooded Delight's pale cheeks, and she answered:

"Yes, it was. I have a cold, and can't go out of my room,--and mother is out,--and--and I was awfully lonesome, so I played I was Cinderella. And then I just happened to think I'd telephone you--just for fun--"

"Have you a stepmother? Is she cruel to you?"

"Mercy, no! Mother is the dearest thing in the world, and she adores me,--spoils me, in fact. She's gone out now to get me some things to make valentines with. But I wish she was here. I thought it would be fun to see,--to see you alone,--but you're so different from what I thought you were."

"Different, how?" said Midget, forgetting her own shyness in her interest in this strange girl.

"Why, you're so--so big, and rosy,--and your eyes snap so."

"You're afraid of me!" exclaimed Midget, laughing merrily.

"I'm not when you laugh like that!" returned Delight, who was beginning to feel more at ease.

"Well, I was afraid of you, too, at first. You looked so--so, breakable, you know."

"Delicate?"

"Yes, fragile. Like those pretty spun sugar things."

"I am delicate. At least, mother says I am. I hate to romp or run, and I'm afraid of people who do those things."

"Well, I'm not afraid of anybody who can play she's Cinderella over a telephone! I love to run and play out-of-doors, but I love to play 'pretend games' too."

"So do I. But I have to play them all by myself. Except sometimes mother plays with me."

"You can play with us. We all play pretend games. Kitty's best at it,--she's my sister. And King--Kingdon, my brother, is grand."

"Take off your things, won't you? I ought to have asked you before. I haven't any sense."

Marjorie jumped up and threw off her hat and coat, tossed them on the couch, and then plumped herself into another big chair near Delight's.

The children were indeed a contrast.

Marjorie, large for her age, full of hearty, healthy life, and irrepressible gayety of spirit, bounced around like a big, good-natured rubber ball. Delight, small, slender, and not very strong, moved always gently and timidly.

Marjorie, too, was dark-haired, dark-eyed, and rosy-cheeked; while Delight was of lovely blonde type, and her pale blue robe suited her, as Midget's crimson cashmere set off her own vivid coloring.

The ice fairly broken, the little girls forgot their shyness, and acquaintance progressed rapidly.

"Have you always lived in New York?" asked Midget.

"Yes; but I'm so delicate mother thinks this place will be better for me. Do you like it here?"

"Why, yes. But I've always lived here, you know. Are you going to school?"

"No; I never go to school. It makes me nervous. I always have a governess at home."

"Oh, how lovely! I'd give anything if I could study that way. Isn't it fun?"

"Oh, no; it's so lonely. I'd ever so much rather go to school and be in a class. But I always faint in a schoolroom."

"I don't faint,--I don't know how. I wish I did, I'd try it, and then Miss Lawrence would have to send me home. Where are you in arithmetic?"

"Partial Payments; but I'm reviewing. Where are you?"

"Cube root, and I hate it."

"So do I. How do you like my room?"

"It's splendid. But I can't take it all in at once."

Marjorie jumped up and walked round the room, stopping to look at the aquarium, the blackboard, the gramophone, and many other modes of entertainment which had been collected to give Delight pleasure.

"Yes, I love my things. I have so many, and father is always bringing me new ones. That's to make up for my being an only child. I often beg mother to adopt a sister for me."

"I'll be your sister," said Midget, in a sudden heartfelt burst of sympathy for the lonely little girl.

"Oh, will you?" she said, wistfully; "and come and live with me?"

"No, not that," laughed Marjorie; "but we'll play we're sisters, and you can call my brother and sisters yours too."

"I'm glad I came to Rockwell," said Delight, with happy eyes; "I think you're splendid."

"And I think you're lovely. I hope we'll get along. Do you squabble?"

"I don't think so," replied Delight, doubtfully; "you see, I never had a chance."

"I don't believe you do. I hate it, myself; but lots of the girls think it's fun to get mad at each other, and stay mad a few weeks and then make up."

"How silly! You're not like that, are you?"

"No, I'm not. I had a friend who used to live in this very house, and we never have been mad at each other in our lives. That's why I didn't say I'd be your friend. It seems sort of--kind of--"

"Yes, I see," said Delight, gently. "You're awfully loyal, aren't you? Well, I'd rather be your sister, anyway,--your play-sister."

"I'll be your step-sister," said Midget, remembering Cinderella. "Not the cross kind."

"No, the pleasant kind. All right, we'll be step-sisters, and will you come to see me often?"

"Yes, and you must come over to my house."

"I will, when mother'll let me. She hates to have me go anywhere."

"Do you know," said Midget, in a spirit of contrition, "I thought you were 'stuck-up.'"

Delight sighed a little. "Everybody thinks that," she said, "just because I don't go to school, and so I don't get acquainted much. But I'm not stuck-up."

"Indeed you're not, and I shall tell all the girls so. But after your cold gets well, you can go out doors to play, can't you?"

"I don't know. Mother never lets me go out much, except with her. Oh, here comes mother now!"

Mrs. Spencer came into the room and smiled pleasantly at Midget.

Delight introduced them, and Marjorie rose and curtseyed, then Mrs. Spencer said:

"I'm glad you came, my dear child. I meant to ask you soon, as I want you and Delight to be great friends."

Mrs. Spencer was an attractive-looking lady and spoke cordially, but somehow Marjorie didn't fancy her.

There was no tangible reason, for she was charming and gracious, but Midget felt she was a nervous, fussy woman, and not calm and capable like her own dear mother.

"My mother is coming to call on you," said Marjorie to her hostess. "I heard her say so. She doesn't know I'm here, for she wasn't at home when I came, but I know she'll be pleased when I tell her."

"Did you come away without mother's permission? Naughty! Naughty!" said Mrs. Spencer, playfully shaking her finger at Marjorie.

Midget's eyes opened wide. "Of course, I shouldn't have come," she said, "if I hadn't known she would be willing." She resented Mrs. Spencer's reproof, as that lady knew nothing of the circumstances, and besides, Marjorie was always allowed to do as she chose afternoons, within certain well-understood restrictions.

But Mrs. Spencer had brought several interesting-looking parcels, and all else was forgotten in the examination of their contents.

They proved to contain gold and silver paper, lace paper, small pictures, crepe paper, cards, ribbons, paste, and lots of other things.

Marjorie's eyes sparkled as she saw the lovely things tumbled out on a low table which Mrs. Spencer drew up in front of the girls. "For valentines?" she exclaimed, as she realized the possibilities.

"Yes; will you help Delight to make them?"

"Indeed, I will, Mrs. Spencer; but not now. It's five o'clock, and I have to go home at five."

"Dear, dear, little girls that run away without mother's permission oughtn't to be so particular about going home on time."

Marjorie was puzzled. Mrs. Spencer didn't see the matter rightly, she was sure, and yet to explain it to her seemed like correcting a grown-up lady, which, of course, was impolite. So she only smiled, and said she must go home, but she would be glad to come again.

To her surprise, Delight began to cry,--not noisily,--but with quiet, steady weeping, that seemed to imply a determination to keep it up.

Marjorie looked her amazement, which was not lessened when Mrs. Spencer said, almost coldly:

"I should think she would cry, poor, dear sick child, when her little friend refuses to stay with her."

"But, Mrs. Spencer," said Midget, really distressed, now, "it is our rule always to go home at five o'clock, unless mother has said we could stay later. So I have to go."

"Very well, then, go on," said Mrs. Spencer, a little pettishly; but she helped Marjorie on with her coat, and patted her on the shoulder.

"You're a good little girl," she said, "and I suppose I'm selfish where Delight is concerned. Will you come again to-morrow morning?"

"Oh, no, thank you; I have to go to school."

"Yes, I suppose you do. Well, come to-morrow afternoon."

"Yes, do," said Delight, staying her tears, as they seemed to do no good.

"I'll see about it," said Midget, a little bewildered by these emotional people. "I'd like to come."

She said her good-byes, and flew across the street to her own home.

She flung to the front door behind her, with what was *almost* a bang, and then throwing her coat and hat on the hall rack, she burst into the living-room, where Mrs. Maynard was sitting with Rosy Posy in her lap.

"Marjorie," her mother said, as she observed the impulsive child, "you are just a shade too noisy. Will you kindly go back to the hall, and try to enter this room in a manner more becoming to a lady and a Maynard?"

"I will, indeed, Mother. And you're quite right; I was awful racketty."

Marjorie returned to the hall, and then came in with graceful, mincing steps, purposely overdoing the scene. She paused in front of her mother dropped an elaborate curtsey, and holding out her hand daintily, said:

"Good-evening, Mrs. Maynard; are you at home?"

"I am, you silly child," said her mother, kissing her affectionately, "and overdone manners are much better than no manners at all."

"Yes'm; and what do you think, Mother? I've been over to see Delight Spencer."

"You have? Why, I meant to take you when I go to call. How did you happen to go?"

So Marjorie told the story of the telephoning, adding: "And you know, Mother, you always used to let me go to Gladys's without asking you, so I went. Wasn't it all right?"

Marjorie looked so disturbed that Mrs. Maynard smiled, and said:

"Why, I suppose there's no harm done,--since the little girl asked you to come--"

Marjorie looked greatly relieved. "Well," she said, "Mrs. Spencer thought it was awful for me to go without asking you,--and then,--she wanted me to stay after five o'clock, and was madder 'n hops 'cause I didn't!"

"What a remarkable lady! But I can judge better if you tell me the whole story."

So Marjorie told all about the afternoon, and Mrs. Maynard was greatly interested.

"Not exactly stuck-up, is she, Midget?" said King, who had come in during the recital.

"No," owned up Marjorie. "I was mistaken about that; and I think I'd like her a lot, if she wasn't the crying kind. I do hate cry babies."

"Ho! You wept oceans when Glad went away."

"Yes," retorted Marjorie, unabashed, "but that's very different. I don't burst into weeps just because a next-door neighbor is going home!"

"'Deed you don't, old girl! You're a brick, and I was a meany to say what I did. But perhaps Delight doesn't cry so much when she's well."

"She's never well. I mean she's delicate and frail and always having colds and things."

"Pooh, a nice sort of girl for you to play with! You're as hardy as an Indian."

"I know it. We all are."

"She probably stays in the house too much," said Mrs. Maynard. "If you children can persuade her to go out of doors and romp with you, she'll soon get stronger."

"She says she hates to romp," observed Marjorie.

"Then I give her up!" cried King. "No stay-in-the-house girls for me. Say, what do you think, Mops! A straw-ride to-morrow afternoon! Mr. Adams is going to take a big sleigh-load of us! Isn't that gay!"

"Fine!" cried Marjorie, the delicate Delight quite forgotten for the moment, "tell me all about it!"

CHAPTER IX
A STRAW-RIDE

T hen, mother," said Marjorie, as she started for school next morning, "you'll call on Mrs. Spencer this morning and ask her to let Delight go on the straw-ride with us this afternoon. Will you, Mother, will you?"

"Yes, my Midget, I told you I would. But I doubt if she'll let the little girl go."

"So do I, but you coax her. Good-bye, Mother."

With a kiss and a squeeze, Marjorie was off, swinging a strap-full of books till they all tumbled on the ground, and then picking them up again.

"I'll help you, Mops," said King, who had followed her down the path. "What a tumble-bug you are!"

"Yes, I am. Say, King, do you believe Delight will go with us?"

"Don't know and don't care. She's a Flossy Flouncy, anyway. Too dressy and fiddle-de-dee for me!"

"Oh, you don't know her. I think she's going to be real nice."

"All right. You can have her. Hi! there's Bunny Black; let's run."

Run they did, and Marjorie flew over the ground quite as fast as Kingdon did.

"Hey, Bunny, wait a minute!" So Bunny waited, and then all three trudged on to school; Marjorie in the middle, while they talked over the fun of the coming sleigh-ride.

Mr. Adams, who was the father of Dorothy, Kitty's chum, took the young people on a straw-ride every winter, if the sleighing happened to be good just at the right time.

The trip was always made out to Ash Grove, the pleasant farm home of Mr. Adams' aunt, and the old lady heartily welcomed the crowd of laughing children that invaded her quiet abode.

After school, Marjorie and King and Kitty ran home to eat a hearty luncheon, and get ready for the great event.

It was a perfect winter day; crisp, clear air, bright sunshine, fine sleighing, and no wind.

"Mothery," called Marjorie, as she entered the house, "where are you?"

"Here I am, dear, in the library. Don't come a like a whirlwind."

"No'm. I'll come in like a gentle summer breeze," and Midget tripped lightly in, waving her skirts as she side-stepped, and greeting her mother with a low bow.

"What about Delight?" she asked, at once, "can she go?"

"Yes, she's going," answered Mrs. Maynard, "but I don't think her mother wants her to go very much. I went over there this morning, and after making my call on the lady, I delivered the invitation for the daughter. Delight was most anxious to go, and coaxed her mother so hard, that Mrs. Spencer finally said yes, though I'm sure it was against her will."

"Is Delight's cold well?"

"I think so, or her mother wouldn't let her go. She'll be more or less in your charge, Marjorie, so do look after her, and don't be thoughtless and heedless."

"How do you like Mrs. Spencer, Mother?"

"She's a very pleasant lady, my dear, and Delight is a beautiful child."

"Yes, isn't she pretty! I'm so glad she's going with us."

The straw-ride was of the real old-fashioned sort.

A big box-sleigh, well filled with clean straw, and with plenty of warm robes, made a cosy nest for a dozen laughing children.

Except for Delight, the Maynards were the last ones to be picked up, and when the jingling sleigh-bells and the chorus of voices was heard, they ran out and were gaily greeted by the others.

"Hop in, Kitty; here, I'll help you. In you go, Midget!" and genial Mr. Adams jumped the girls in, while King climbed over the side by himself. Then Mr. Adams went back to his seat beside the driver, and they crossed the street to call for Delight.

She was watching at the window, and came out as the sleigh drove up.

She was so bundled up in wraps and scarfs and veils, that they could scarcely see her face at all, but Marjorie introduced her to the others, and then Delight cuddled down in the straw close to Marjorie's side.

"Isn't it strange?" she whispered. "I never saw a sleigh before without seats in it. Won't we fall out?"

"No, indeed!" answered King, heartily; "that's just what we won't do. Unless when we strike a bump."

Just then they did "strike a bump," and Delight was almost frightened at the jounce she received.

"Oh," she exclaimed, "it--it takes your breath away,--but--but I think it's very nice."

"Plucky girl!" said King, and as that was the highest compliment he could pay a girl, Marjorie felt a thrill of pleasure that King was going to like Delight after all.

"I think you'd like it better without that awful thick veil over your face," King went on. "You can't see the snow through that, can you?"

"No, I can't," said Delight, and she pulled off her veil, leaving her roseleaf face, with its crown of golden curls exposed to view. A hood of white swansdown was tied under her chin with white ribbons, and her smile, though shy, was very sweet.

"That's better!" cried King, approvingly. "Now we can see what you say. Whoo-oo!!"

King blew a sudden blast on a tin horn which he drew from his pocket, and as all the boys in the sleigh, and some of the girls did the same, the noise was deafening.

Delight looked startled, and no wonder, but Marjorie reassured her by saying:

"Don't let that scare you. It's the signal that we've crossed the city limits. They always toot when we cross the line. I don't, 'cause I hate to blow a horn, and anyway, there's noise enough without me."

"I should say there was!" said Delight, for the boys were still tooting now and then, and there was gay laughter and shouting.

"Haven't you ever been on a straw-ride before?" asked Ethel Frost, who sat the other side of Delight.

"No, I never have. I've always lived in the city."

"Stuck-up!" thought Ethel, but she said nothing. It was a peculiar but deep-seated notion among the Rockwell children, that any one from the city would look down on them and their simple pleasures, and they foolishly, but none the less strongly resented it.

And so, poor Delight had unwittingly said the worst thing she could say by way of her own introduction.

"Do you like the city best?" said Harry Frost, who sat opposite the girls.

"I don't know yet," said Delight, honestly; "it's all so different here."

This was not helping matters, and Harry only said "Huh!" and turned to talk to King.

Ethel, too, seemed uninterested in the city girl, and as Marjorie felt herself, in a way, responsible for the little stranger, she spoke up, loyally:

"Of course she can't tell yet, but of course she will like Rockwell as soon as she gets more used to it, and if she doesn't like the Rockwell boys and girls, it'll be their own fault. So there, now!"

"I do like them," said Delight, with her shy little smile; "and I think I can get used to those awful horns that they blow."

"Good for you, Flossy Flouncy!" cried King, and the nickname so suited the pretty, dainty little girl, that it clung to her ever after.

But though she tried, Delight couldn't seem to adopt the ways of the other children. They were a hearty, rollicking crowd, full of good-natured chaff, and boisterous nonsense, and Delight, who had lived much alone, was bewildered at their noise and fun.

But she slipped her hand from her pretty white muff, and tucked it into Marjorie's, who gave her a squeeze that meant sympathy and encouragement.

Midget was beginning to realize that the more she saw of Delight, the better she liked her. And the brave way in which the little girl met the coolness and indifference that were shown her, roused Marjorie's sense of justice, and she at once began to stand up for her.

And when Marjorie Maynard stood up for anybody, it meant a great deal to the youthful population of Rockwell. For Midget was a general favorite, and since Gladys was gone there were several girls who would gladly have stepped into her place in Marjorie's affections. They had begged to share her desk at school, but Midget didn't want any one to do that, so she still sat alone each day.

And now, she had this new girl under her wing, and she was beginning to make it felt that she was Delight's champion, and the others could act accordingly.

"Do you like coasting?" said Ethel Frost, as they passed a fine hill dotted with boys and girls and sleds.

"Yes, I love it!" replied Delight, her blue eyes sparkling as she watched the sleds fly downhill.

"Why, Flossy Flouncy!" cried King; "you couldn't go coasting! I don't believe you've ever tried it!"

"I never did but once," said Delight, "and then the hill wasn't very good, but it was fun. I'd love to go on a hill like that."

"Would your mother let you?" said Marjorie doubtfully.

"No, I don't believe she would. But I'd coax her till she had to."

"That's right," said King. "We'll go to-morrow, and then you'll see what real coasting is."

It was not a very long ride to their destination, and at last the sleigh turned in at a farm entrance and passed through a long winding avenue of trees to the house.

It was an old yellow farmhouse, big and capacious, and in the doorway stood a smiling-faced little old lady awaiting them.

This was Miss Adams, Dorothy's grand-aunt, and called Auntie Adams by all the children who visited her. They all tumbled out of the sleigh, and ran laughing into the house.

Each was greeted by Miss Adams, and cries of "Where's Ponto?" and "Oh, here's Polly!" and "Hello, Tabby," were heard.

"This is Delight Spencer," said Marjorie, as she presented her to Miss Adams; "she's a new friend of mine, and Mr. Adams said I might bring her."

"I'm very glad to see you, my dear," said Miss Adams, kissing the wistful little face; "you are welcome to the old farm."

"I've never seen a farmhouse before," said Delight, as she glanced round at the old mahogany furniture and brass candlesticks shining in the firelight from the big fireplace; "and, oh, isn't it beautiful!"

Miss Adams was much pleased at this honest compliment to her old home, and she patted Delight's shoulder, as she said: "I'm sure we shall be great friends, you and I. Run away now, with Marjorie, and lay off your wraps in the north bed-room."

The girls went up the short turning staircase, and into a quaint old-fashioned bedroom, with four-poster bed, chintz hangings, and fine old carved furniture.

"Isn't it strange?" said Delight, looking about. "I suppose the ladies who used to live here are dead and gone. I mean, the old ancestors of Miss Adams. Let's play we're them, Marjorie. You be Priscilla and I'll be Abigail."

"Not very pretty names," said Midget, doubtfully.

"Oh, yes, they are. I'll call you Prissy and you call me Abby. I'll be knitting, and you can be spinning on that spinning-wheel."

The others had gone downstairs, but forgetting all about them, Delight sat herself stiffly in one of the high-backed old chairs, and knitted industriously, with invisible yarn and only her own slender little fingers for needles.

Always ready for make-believe play Marjorie sat at the spinning-wheel,--on the wrong side, to be sure, but that didn't matter.

"Are you going to the ball at Squire Harding's?" said Delight, in a prim voice.

"Yes, that I am," said Marjorie. "Half the county will be there. I shall wear my blue brocade, with collar of pearls."

"How fair thou wilt look! I have but my crimson taffeta turned and made over. But I have a new wimple."

"What is a wimple, Delight?"

"I don't know exactly, but they wore them once. We're not sisters you know, I'm just calling on you; I'm quite poor. Ah, Prissy, I would I could achieve a new gown for the ball. My lady Calvert will be there, and she is of the quality, forsooth."

"Aye, Abby, but thou art more beautiful in thy ragged garb, than she in her stiff satins."

"Sayest thou so? Thou dost but flatter. But among all my noble ancestors, the Adamses, there was never a woman aught but fair; or a man aught but brave!"

Delight said this in a high, stilted voice, and as she sat primly in the straight-backed old chair, knitting away at nothing, she presented a funny, attractive little picture.

Miss Adams, who had come in search of the girls, paused at the door, and heard Delight's words.

"You dear child!" she cried; "you dramatic small person! What are you two doing?"

"We fell to playing, Miss Adams," said Marjorie, "and we forgot to go downstairs."

"We couldn't help it," supplemented Delight. "This old room and dear old furniture just made me think I really was a Colonial Dame, so we played we were."

"You're a treasure!" said Miss Adams, clasping Delight in her arms. "As for Midget, here, she's always been my treasure, too. I think some day you two little girls must come and visit me, all by yourselves, will you?"

"Yes, indeed we will."

"But now, come downstairs, and join the games down there."

Down they went, and found the gay party playing Fox and Geese.

Marjorie was an adaptable nature, and equally well pleased with any game, so she flung herself into the circle, and ran about as gaily as any one. But Delight shrank away from the frolic, and asked to be allowed to look on.

"No, indeed, Flossy Flouncy!" cried Harry Frost. "You must play our games, if you want us to like you. Come on, we won't hurt you."

"Come on in, the water's fine!" called King, and Delight reluctantly took the place assigned her.

She tried to do as the others did, but long practice had made them alert and skillful, while she was inexperienced at such sports. She became bewildered at the quick changes of position, and as a result was soon caught, and had to be the "Fox."

Then the situation was hopeless, for it was impossible for Delight to catch any of the quick-witted and quick-moving "geese," who darted in and out, tapping her shoulder, when she should have tapped theirs, and teasing her for being slow.

They were not intentionally rude, these gay-spirited young people, but a girl who couldn't play Fox and Geese seemed to them a justifiable butt for ridicule. Determined to succeed, Delight ran from one to another, arriving just too late every time. The unfamiliar exercise wearied her, her cheeks glowed pink with mortification at her repeated failures, and her breath came quickly, but she was plucky and kept up her brave efforts.

Kingdon saw this, and admired the spirit she showed.

"Look here, Flossy Flouncy," he said, not unkindly, "you've been Fox long enough; now I'll be Fox, and you sit down on the sofa and get rested."

Delight looked at him gratefully, and without a word she went and sat on the sofa and Miss Adams came and sat by her and put her arm round the trembling child. Soon after this, the game was stopped because supper was announced.

Delight sat between Marjorie and King, and though she ate but little she enjoyed seeing the delicious country viands that were served.

Little chicken pies, a whole one to each person; flaky biscuits, and golden butter; home-made ice cream and many sorts of home-made cakes and jellies and preserves. The hungry children disposed of an enormous quantity of these pleasant things, but Miss Adams was not surprised at their appetites, for this was an annual experience with her. After supper, they sang songs. Miss Adams sat at her old-fashioned square piano, and played some well-known songs in which they all joined.

"I heard a song on a phonograph, the other day," said Harry Frost; "it was about a bonnie lassie. Do you know that, Miss Adams?"

"No, dear boy, I don't. I'm sorry. Can't you sing it without the piano?"

"No, I don't know it. But I'd like to hear it again."

"I know it," said Delight, timidly. "If you want me to, I'll sing it."

She looked so shy and sweet, that there was nothing forward about her offer, merely a desire to please.

"Do, my dear," said Miss Adams, giving her place to the child.

Delight sat down at the piano, and striking a few chords, began: "I know a lassie, a bonnie, bonnie lassie," and sang it through in a sweet, childish voice.

"That's it!" cried Harry, as she finished. "Jiminy! but you're a singer, all right."

There was much applause, and requests for more songs, but Delight, overcome by attracting so much attention, turned bashful again and couldn't be persuaded to sing any more.

However, it was time to go home, so they all bundled into their wraps again, and clambered into the sleigh. Delight was quiet all the way home, and sat with her hand clasped close in Marjorie's.

"Good-night," she whispered, as she got out at her own house. "Good-night, Marjorie dear. I thank you for a pleasant time, but I don't believe I want to go again."

"Oh, yes, you will," Marjorie whispered back. "Don't be so easily discouraged."

CHAPTER X
MAKING VALENTINES

Now, what do you think of a girl like that?" Marjorie exclaimed, as she finished a description of Delight's behavior on the straw-ride.

"I think she's a little lady," said Mr. Maynard, with a twinkle of amusement in his eye, "and she was pretty well frightened by the noisy fun of the Rockwell young people."

"But, Father," said King, "we didn't do anything wrong, or even rude, but of course, you can't go on a straw-ride and sit as still as if you were in church, can you?"

"No," said Mrs. Maynard, taking up King's cause; "children are meant to be noisy, especially on a sleighing party. But I wouldn't worry about the little Spencer girl. If she continues to live here, she can't help doing as you young Romans do, after a time."

"Ho!" cried King. "Imagine Flossy Flouncy tumbling around like our Midget. Hi, there, sister, you're it!"

King clapped Marjorie on the back and then ran around the dining-table, from which they had all just risen.

"Kit's it!" cried Marjorie, clapping Kitty in turn.

"Nope, I had my fingers crossed," said Kitty, exhibiting her twisted digits, and calmly walking out of the room, her arm through her father's.

"All right, I'll catch you, King," and Marjorie made a dive for him.

He was wary, and just as she nearly touched him, he stooped and slid under the table. After him went Midget, and of course, scrambled under just as King dodged up on the other side.

Out came Marjorie, flying after King, who raced up the front stairs and down the back ones, landing in the kitchen with a wild shriek of, "Hide me, Ellen, she's after me!"

"Arrah, ye bletherin' childher!" cried Ellen, "ye're enough to set a saint crhazy wid yer rally poosin'! In there wid ye, now!"

The good-natured Irishwoman pushed King in a small cupboard, and stood with her back against the door.

"What'll ye have, Miss Marjorie?" she said, as Midget rushed in half a minute later.

"Where's King?" asked Marjorie, breathless and panting.

"Masther King, is it? I expict he's sthudyin' his schoolbooks like the little gin-tleman he is. Shkip out, now, Miss Marjorie, dear, I must be doin' me work."

"All right, Ellen, go on and do it. Go on now, why don't you? Why don't you, Ellen? Do you have to stand against that door to keep it shut?"

"Yes, Miss, the,--the lock is broke, sure."

"Oh, is it? Well, you go on to your work, and I'll hold the door shut for a while."

"Och, I cuddent think of throublin' ye, Miss. Run on, now, happen yer mother is wantin' ye."

"Happen she isn't. Scoot, Ellen, and give me a chance at that door."

Unable to resist Midget's wheedling glance, the big Irishwoman moved away from the door, and Marjorie threw it open, and disclosed King, calmly sitting on a flour barrel.

As he was fairly caught, the game was over, and the two, with intertwined arms rejoined the family.

"Good race?" said Mr. Maynard, looking at the exhausted runners.

"Fine!" said Marjorie. "You see, Father, Delight has no brothers or sisters, so how could she be very racketty? She couldn't play tag with her mother or father, could she?"

"I think you'd play tag with the Pope of Rome, if you couldn't get any one else."

"That would be rather fun," said Midget, laughing, "only I s'pose his robes and things would trip him up. But I do believe he'd like it. I don't 'spect he has much fun, anyway. Does he?"

"Not of that sort, probably. But, Midget mine, there are other sorts of fun beside tearing up and down stairs like a wild Indian."

"Yes, and one sort is playing 'Authors'; come on, and have a game, will you, Father?"

"I'll give you half an hour," said Mr. Maynard, looking at his watch. "That's all I can spare for my wild Indians this evening."

"Goody!" cried Midget, "half an hour is quite a lot. Come on, King and Kit. Will you play, Mother?"

"Not now, I have some things I must attend to. I'll take Father's place when his half-hour is up."

So they settled down to "Authors," which was one of their favorite games, and of which they never tired. "Delight would like this," said Marjorie, as she took a trick; "she's fond of quiet games. Mother, may I go over to-morrow afternoon and make valentines with her?"

"Yes, if you like, dearie," replied Mrs. Maynard.

"May I go, too?" said Kitty.

"No, Kitty, I want you at home to-morrow. The seamstress will be cutting your new frock, and you must be here to try it on when she wants you."

"All right, Mother. May I ask Dorothy here, then?"

"Yes, if you like. But you must stay in the house."

"Yes'm, we will."

The Maynards were obedient children, and though sometimes disappointed, never demurred at their parents' decrees. They had long ago learned that such demurring would do no good, and that to obey pleasantly made things pleasanter all round.

After luncheon the next day, Marjorie got ready to go to spend the afternoon with Delight.

She wore her new plaid dress trimmed with black velvet and gilt buttons, and as red was the prevailing color in the plaid, her dark curls were tied up with a big red bow.

Very pretty she looked as she came for her mother's inspection.

"Am I all right, Mother?"

"Yes, Midget mine; you look as spick and span as a nice little Queen of Sheba.

Now don't slide down the banisters, or do anything hoydenish. Try to behave more as Delight does."

"Oh, I'm bound to be good over there. And making valentines is nice, quiet work. May I stay till six, Mother?"

"No, come home at half-past five. That's late enough for little Queens of Sheba to stay away from their mothers."

"All right, I'll skip at five-thirty. Good-bye, Mothery dearie."

With a kiss and a squeeze Marjorie was off, and Mrs. Maynard watched her from the window, until she disappeared through the Spencers' doorway.

"I'm so glad to see you!" said Delight, as Marjorie came dancing into her room. "Everything's all ready. You sit over there."

So Midget sat down opposite her friend at a long, low table, on which were all the valentine materials laid out in readiness.

"What beautiful things," cried Midget; "but I don't know how to make valentines."

"I'll show you. It's awfully easy, and lots of fun."

It was easy for Delight. Her deft little fingers pinched up bits of tissue paper into charming little rosebuds or forget-me-nots, and her dainty taste chose lovely color combinations.

Marjorie's quick wits soon caught the idea, and though not quite so nimble-fingered as Delight, she soon showed an inventive originality that devised novel ideas.

Sometimes they only took the round or square lace papers, and mounted them on cards, and added little scrap pictures of doves or cupids or flowers.

Then some of them were quite different. Delight cut a heart-shaped piece of cardboard, and round the edge dabbled an irregular border of gold paint. The inside she tinted pink all over, and on it wrote a loving little verse in gilt letters.

This, though simple, was such a pretty card, that Marjorie made one like it, adding a garland of roses across it, which made it prettier still.

Then they made pretty ones of three panel cards. To do this they took an oblong card, and cut it half through with a penknife in such a way that it divided the card into three parts, the outside two shutting over the middle one like window blinds over a window.

The card would stand up like a screen, and they decorated each panel with posies and verses.

"What are you going to do with all these valentines?" asked Midget, as they were busily working away at them.

"Half are yours," said Delight, "and half are mine. We can each send them wherever we please. Of course I'll send most of mine to friends in New York; I haven't any friends here."

"Indeed you have!" cried Midget. "Don't be silly. You've three Maynard friends, to begin with; and all the boys and girls are your friends, only you don't know them yet. I'll tell you what to do. You send valentines to all the Rockwell children,--I mean all our crowd, and they'll just love 'em. Will you?"

"Why, yes, if you think I can when I don't know them very well. I can easily make enough for them and my New York set too."

"Yes, do; I'll help you, if I get mine done first. And anyway, it's 'most two weeks before Valentine's day."

"Oh, there's plenty of time. Look, isn't this a pretty one?"

Delight held up a card on which she had painted with her water colors a clouded blue sky effect. And on it, in a regular flight, she had pasted tiny birds that she found among the scrap pictures.

"Lovely!" said Midget; "you ought to have a verse about birds on it."

"I don't know any verse about birds, do you?"

"No; let's make one up."

"Yes, we could do that. It ought to go some-thing like this: 'The swallows tell that Spring is here, so flies my heart to you, my dear.'"

"Yes, that's nice and valentiny,--but it isn't Spring in February."

"No, but that's poetic. Valentines have to be love-poems, and Spring is 'most always in a love-poem."

"Yes, I s'pose it is. I'd like to do some funny ones. I'm not much good at sentimental poetry. I guess I'll do one for King. Here's a picture of a bird carrying a ring in its beak. Ring rhymes with King, you know."

"Oh, yes, make one of those limerick things: 'There was a young fellow named King,--'"

"That's the kind I mean. Write that down while I paste. Then write: 'Who sent to his lady a ring.' Now what next?"

"Something like this: 'He said, "Sweet Valentine, I pray you be mine." And she answered him, "No such a thing!"'"

"Oh, that's a good one. Do send that to your brother. But it hasn't much sense to it."

"No, they never have. Now, I'll make one for Kit: 'There was a dear girlie named Kit, who was having a horrible fit.'"

"That isn't a bit valentiny."

"No, I know it. This is a funny one. We'll make her another pretty one. 'When they said, "Are you better?" she wrote them a letter in which she replied, "Not a bit!"'"

"I think that's sort of silly," said Delight, looking at the rhymes she had written at Midget's dictation.

"Yes, I know it is," returned Marjorie, cheerfully. "It's nonsense, and that's 'most always silly. But Kit loves it, and so do I. We make up awful silly rhymes sometimes. You don't know Kitty very well yet, do you? She's only ten, but she plays pretend games lovely. Better'n I do. She has such gorgeous language. I don't know where she gets it."

"It comes," said Delight, with a far-away look in her eyes. "I have it too. You can't remember that you've ever heard it anywhere; the words just come of themselves."

"But you must have heard them, or read them," said practical Midget.

"Yes, I suppose so. But it doesn't seem like memory. It's just as if you had always known them. Sometimes I pretend all to myself. And I'm a princess."

"I knew you would be! Kit said so too. She likes to be a princess. But I like to be a queen. You might as well be, you know, when you're just pretending."

"Yes, you'd be a splendid queen. You're so big and strong. But I like to be a princess, and 'most always I'm captive, in a tower, waiting for somebody to rescue me."

"Come on, let's play it now," said Marjorie, jumping up. "I'm tired of pasting things, and we can finish these some other day. You be a captive princess, and I'll be a brave knight coming to rescue you."

But just then Mrs. Spencer appeared, carrying a tray on which were glasses of milk, crackers, and dear little cakes, and the two girls concluded they would postpone their princess play till a little later.

"I'm so bothered," said Mrs. Spencer, in her tired, plaintive voice, as she sat down with the children; "I cannot get good servants to stay with me here. I had no trouble in the city at all. Does your mother have good servants, Marjorie?"

"Yes, Mrs. Spencer, I think so. They're the ones we've always had."

"Well, mine wouldn't come with me from the city, so I had to get some here. And the cook has a small child, and to-day he's ill,--really quite ill,--and the waitress is helping the cook, and so I had to bring up this tray myself."

"Can't I help you in some way, Mrs. Spencer?" asked Marjorie, impulsively. It was her nature to be helpful, though it would never have occurred to Delight to make such an offer.

"No, dear child; there's nothing you could do. But the doctor is down there now, to see the little one, and I fear if the child is very ill, cook will have to leave, and what to do then, I don't know."

"Perhaps the child is only a little sick," said Midge, who wanted to be comforting, but did not know quite what to say to comfort a grown-up lady.

"We'll soon know, after the doctor makes his decision," said Mrs. Spencer. "Oh, that's Maggie crying. I'm afraid it's a bad case."

Sure enough, sounds of loud sobbing could be heard from the direction of the kitchen, and Mrs. Spencer hurried away to learn what had happened.

"It must be awful," said Marjorie, "to be a cook and have your little boy ill, and no time to attend to him, because you have to cook for other people."

Delight stared at her.

"I think the awful part," she said, "is to have your cook's baby get ill, so she can't cook your dinner."

"Delight, that is selfish, and I don't think you ought to talk so."

"I don't think it's selfish to want the services of your own servants. That's what you have them for,--to cook and work for you. They oughtn't to let their little boys get sick."

"I don't suppose they do it on purpose," said Midge, half laughing and half serious; "but I'm sorry for your cook anyway."

"I'm sorry for *us*! But, gracious, Marjorie, hear her cry! The little boy must be awfully sick!"

"Yes, indeed! She's just screaming! Shall we go down?"

"No, I'm sure mother wouldn't like us to. But I don't feel like playing princess, do you?"

"No, not while she screams like that. There goes the doctor away."

From the window, the girls saw the doctor hasten down the path, jump into his electric runabout, and whiz rapidly away.

They could still hear sobbing from the kitchen, and now and then the moans of the baby.

At last, Mary, the waitress, came to take the tray away.

"What is the matter with Maggie's little boy, Mary?" asked Delight.

"He's sick, Miss Delight."

"But why does Maggie scream so?"

"It's near crazy she is, fearin' he'll die."

"Oh," said Marjorie, "is he as bad as that! What's the matter with him, Mary?"

"He,--he has a cold, Miss."

"But babies don't die of a cold! Is that all that ails him?"

"He has,--he has a fever, Miss."

"A high fever, I s'pose. Rosy Posy had that when she had croup. Is it croup, Mary?"

"No, Miss,--I don't know, Miss, oh, don't be askin' me!"

With a flurried gesture, Mary took the tray and left the room.

"It's very queer," said Delight, "they're making an awful fuss over a sick baby. Here's the doctor back again, and another man with him."

The two men came in quickly, and Mrs. Spencer met them at the front door. They held a rapid consultation, and then the doctor went to the telephone and called up several different people to whom he talked one after another.

And then Mrs. Spencer went to the telephone.

"Oh," said Delight, looking at Marjorie with startled eyes, "she's calling up father in New York. It must be something awful!"

CHAPTER XI
MARJORIE CAPTIVE

I t *was* something awful. The doctor diagnosed the child's case as diphtheria, and proceeded at once to take the steps ordered by the Board of Health in such cases.

Mrs. Spencer wanted to send the little one to the hospital, but Doctor Mendel said that would not be allowed. So the house was to be disinfected, and a strict quarantine maintained until all danger should be past.

"The woman and her child must be put in certain rooms, and not allowed to leave them," said the doctor; "and no one in the house must go out of it, and no one out of it may come in."

"What!" cried Mrs. Spencer, in dismay, thinking of Marjorie. And Marjorie and Delight, unable to keep away any longer, came into the room just in time to hear the doctor's statement.

"What's the matter, mother?" cried Delight. "Tell me about it! Is Maggie's little boy going away?"

"You tell her, Doctor Mendel," said Mrs. Spencer; I can't."

"Why, Marjorie Maynard?" exclaimed the doctor, "are you here? Well, this is a pretty kettle of fish!"

Although the Spencers had never seen Doctor Mendel before, he was the Maynards' family physician, and he realized at once the great misfortune of Marjorie's presence in the infected house.

"Yes, I'm here," said Midget; "can't I go home?"

"No, child," said Doctor Mendel, gravely; "you cannot leave this house until all danger of infection is over. That will be two weeks at least, and perhaps more."

"And can't Mr. Spencer come home?" asked Mrs. Spencer.

"No; unless he stays here after he comes in. He can not go back and forth to New York every day."

Mrs. Spencer looked utterly bewildered. Accustomed to depend upon her husband in any emergency, she felt quite unable to meet this situation.

"And there is danger of these two girls having diphtheria?" she said, in a scared voice, as if anxious to know the worst at once.

"There is grave danger, Mrs. Spencer, for all in the house. But we will hope by careful treatment to avoid that. The quarantine, however, is imperative. You must not let your servants or your family go out into the street, nor must you allow any one except myself to come in."

"Oh, Doctor Mendel," cried Marjorie, "how can I see Mother?"

"You can't see her. I'm sorry, Marjorie, but you simply can not go home, nor can she come here."

"And I'll have to have diphtheria, and die, without seeing her at all!"

"Tut, tut! You're not going to have diphtheria, I hope. These precautions are necessary, because of the law, but you're by no means sure to take the disease."

"Delight will," said Mrs. Spencer, in a hopeless tone. "She's so delicate, and so subject to throat affections. Oh, how can I stand all this without any one to help me? Can't I have a trained nurse?"

Doctor Mendel almost laughed at the lady's request.

"Of course you may, as soon as there's a patient for her to take care of. But you surely don't want one when there's no illness in this part of the house."

"Why, so there isn't!" said Mrs. Spencer, looking greatly relieved. "I'm so bewildered I felt that these two children were already down with diphtheria."

"It's a very trying situation," went on Doctor Mendel, looking kindly at Mrs. Spencer. "For I do not see how your husband can come home, if he wants to continue at his business. And surely, there's no use of his coming home, so long as there's no illness in your immediate family. He would better stay in New York."

"Oh, not in New York," cried Mrs. Spencer. "He can come to Rockwell every night, and stay at the hotel or some place."

"Yes, that would be better; then you can telephone often."

"And I can telephone to Mother!" said Midget, who was beginning to see a brighter side.

"Yes, of course," agreed the doctor. "I'll go there, and tell her all about it."

"Won't she be surprised!"

"Yes, I fancy she will! Do you want her to send you some clothes?"

"Why, yes; I s'pose so. I never thought of that! Oh, I'd rather go home!"

The bright side suddenly faded, and Midget's curly head went down in her arm, and she shook with sobs. A vision of home, and the dear family around the dinner-table, while she was exiled in a strange house, was too much for her.

"Now, Marjorie," said the doctor, "you must bear this bravely. It is hard, I know, but Mrs. Spencer is by far the greatest sufferer. Here she is, with two children to look after, and her husband shut out from his home, and her servants in a state of unreasoning terror. I think you two girls should brace up, and help Mrs. Spencer all you can."

"I think so, t-too," said Midget, in a voice still choking with tears, and then Delight began to cry.

Her crying wasn't a sudden outburst like Marjorie's, but a permanent sort of affair, which she pursued diligently and without cessation.

Mrs. Spencer paid little attention to the two weeping children, for the poor lady had other responsibilities that required her attention.

"What about Maggie, Doctor?" she asked.

"She must stay here, of course. And, as she can't go to a hospital, she will probably prefer to stay here. Your waitress may desert you, but I will tell her if she goes, it is in defiance of the law, and she will be punished. I trust, Mrs. Spencer, that there will be no more illness here, and the worst will be the inconvenience of this quarantine. At any rate we will look at it that way, so long as there are no signs of infection. Now, I will go over to the Maynards and explain matters to them, and I will meet Mr. Spencer at the train, and he will telephone you at once. Meantime, I will myself superintend the disinfection of this house. And remember, while there is danger for the two little girls, I do not think it probable that they will be affected."

"I hope not," said Mrs. Spencer, sighing. "And here's another thing, Doctor. I expect a governess for Delight, a Miss Hart, who is to come with Mr. Spencer on the train this evening. She should be warned."

"Yes, indeed. I'll meet them at the train, and attend to that for you. Probably she'll remain at the hotel over night, and go back to the city to-morrow."

"She could go to our house to stay," said Marjorie. She was still crying, but she loved to make plans. "Then she could telephone the lessons over to Delight, and I could learn a little too. Oh, I won't have to go to school for two weeks!"

This was a consolation, and the happy thought entirely stopped Marjorie's tears.

Not so Delight. She cried on, softly, but steadily, until Midget looked at her with real curiosity.

"What do you cry that way for, Delight?" she said. "It doesn't do any good."

Delight looked at her, but wept industriously on.

"Oh, come," said Midget, "let's look for the bright side. Let's pretend I've come to visit you for two weeks, and let's have some fun out of this thing."

"How can you talk so?" said Delight, through her tears. "We may both be dead in two weeks."

"Nonsense!" cried Doctor Mendel; "no more of that sort of talk! If you're so sure of having diphtheria, I'll send you to the hospital at once."

Delight did not know the doctor as well as Marjorie did, and this suggestion frightened her.

She tried to stop crying, and smile, and she succeeded fairly well.

"That's better," said the doctor. "Now, I'm going across the street. Marjorie, what message do you want to send your mother? Of course she'll send over some clothes and things. You can have anything you want sent, but don't have needless things, for they must all be disinfected later, and it might harm your best clothes."

"Oh, I shan't want my best clothes, since we can't have company or parties," said Midget, interested now, in spite of herself. "Tell Mother to send my night things; and my red cashmere for to-morrow morning, and my other red hair ribbons, and my pink kimono, and my worsted slippers, and that book on my bureau, the one with the leaf turned down, and some handkerchiefs, and--"

"There, there, child, I can't remember those things, and your mother will know, anyway,--except about the book with the leaf turned down,--I'll tell her that. And you can telephone her, you know."

"Oh, so I can! That will be almost like seeing her. Can't I telephone now?"

"No, I'd rather tell her about it myself. Then I'll tell her to call you up, and you can give her your list of hair ribbons and jimcracks."

"All right then. Hurry up, Doctor, so I can talk to her soon."

Doctor Mendel went away, and Marjorie and Delight sat and looked at each other. Mrs. Spencer had gone to the kitchen to arrange for the comfort of the distressed mother, and the little girls were trying to realize what had happened.

"I'm glad you're here," said Delight, "for I'd be terribly lonely without you, in all this trouble."

Midget was silent. She couldn't honestly say she was glad she was there, and yet to say she was sorry seemed unkind.

"Well, as long as I am here," she said at last, "I'm glad you're glad. It's all so strange! To be here staying in Gladys's house, and Gladys not here, and I can't get away even if I want to,--why, I can't seem to get used to it."

"It's awful!" said Mrs. Spencer, coming in from the kitchen. "I hope your mother won't blame me, Marjorie; I'm sure I couldn't help it."

"Of course she won't blame you, Mrs. Spencer. She'll only be sorry for you."

"But she'll be so worried about you."

"Yes'm; I s'pose she will. But maybe, if I do take it, it will be a light case."

"Oh, don't talk of light cases! I hope you won't have it at all,--either of you."

After what seemed to Marjorie a long time of waiting, her mother called her up on the telephone.

"My dear little girl," said Mrs. Maynard, "how shall I get along without you for two weeks?"

"Oh, Mother," said Marjorie, "you have the others, but I haven't anybody! How shall I get along without you?"

Marjorie's voice was trembling, and though Mrs. Maynard was heart-broken she forced herself to be cheerful for Midget's sake.

"Well, dearie," she said, "we must make the best of it. I'll telephone you three times a day,--or at least, some of us will,--and I'll write you letters."

"Oh, will you, Mother? That will be lovely!"

"Yes, I'll write you every day. You can receive letters although you can't send any. Now, I want you to be my own brave little daughter, and not only try to be cheerful and pleasant yourself, but cheer up Mrs. Spencer and Delight."

"Yes, Mother, I will try. I feel better already, since I've heard your voice."

"Of course you do. And Father will talk to you when he comes home, and to-morrow Kitty and King can talk, and you'll almost feel as if you were at home."

"Yes,--but oh, Mother, it's awful, isn't it?"

"No, it isn't awful at all, unless you get ill But we won't cross that bridge until we come to it. Now, I'll send over a suitcase to-night, and then I can send more things to-morrow."

"Yes, Mother. And put in your picture, won't you? The one on my mantelpiece, I mean. Then I'll have it to kiss good-night to."

Mrs. Maynard's voice choked a little, but she said:

"Yes, dear, I will. Good-bye for now; we mustn't monopolize Mrs. Spencer's telephone."

"Good-bye," said Midget, reluctantly, and hung up the receiver, feeling that now she was indeed an exile from her home. But not long after, she was called to the telephone again, and her father's cheery voice said:

"Why, Marjorie Midget Mopsy Maynard! What's this I hear about your deserting your home and family?"

"Oh, Father dear, isn't it terrible!"

"Why, I don't know as it is. You'll have a fine visit with your little friend, and you won't have to go to school, and I should think you'd have a fine time! But some people are never satisfied!"

"Now, don't tease, Father. You know I'll just go crazy with homesickness to see you all again!"

"Oh, well, if you really do go crazy, I'll put you in a nice pretty little lunatic asylum that I know of. But before your mind is entirely gone, I want you to have a good time with Delight, and I'll help all I can."

"I don't see how you can help much, if I can't see you."

"You don't, eh? Well, you'll find out, later on. But just now, I'm going to give you three rules, and I want you to obey them. Will you?"

"Of course I will, Father. What are they?"

"First, never think for a moment that you're going to catch that sore throat that the cook's little boy has. I don't think you are, and I don't want to think so. Promise?"

"Yes, I promise. What next?"

"Next; never think that you're to stay over there two weeks. Never use the words at all. Just think each day, that you're merely staying that one night, and that you're just staying for fun. See?"

"Yes; I'll promise, but it won't be easy."

"Make it easy then. I'll help you. And third, don't feel sorry for yourself."

"Oh, Father, I do!"

"Well, don't! If you want to feel sorry for somebody, choose some one else, a poor Hottentot, or a lame kangaroo, or even your old father. But, mind, it's a rule, you're not to feel sorry for Marjorie Maynard."

"That's a funny rule. But I'll try to mind it."

"That's my own dear daughter. Now, to begin. As you're to stay with Delight to-night, we're sending over your night things. Go to bed early and sleep well, so you can wake bright and fresh and have fun playing all day to-morrow."

All this sounded so gay and pleasant that Marjorie was really very much cheered up, and replied gaily:

"All right, Daddy; I'll do just as you say. And will you call me up to-morrow morning before you go to New York?"

"Yes, of course I will. Now, good-night,--just the same as a good-night at home."

"Good-night, Father," and Midget hung up the receiver again.

By this time Delight had stopped her crying, and Mrs. Spencer had become a little more resigned to the unpleasant state of things. The servants had consented to stay, for the present, and their decision was more due to Doctor Mendel's hints about the law, than their own loyalty to Mrs. Spencer.

Then Doctor Mendel had met Mr. Spencer at the railroad station, and had explained affairs to him.

Although it seemed very hard it was thought advisable by all interested, that Mr. Spencer should not go to his home at all. His business, which was large and important, required his presence every day, and to take two weeks away from it just at that time would be disastrous in effect.

Mr. Maynard, who was present at the interview, invited Mr. Spencer to stay at his home until the quarantine should be raised, and this offer of hospitality was gratefully accepted.

"It seems only fair," said Mr. Maynard, "that we should entertain you, as you have our Marjorie as a guest at your house."

"An unwilling guest, I fear," said Mr. Spencer, with a sad smile.

"But ready to make the best of it, as we all must be," rejoined Mr. Maynard.

CHAPTER XII
MISS HART HELPS

Miss Hart, Delight's new governess, who came out from New York with Mr. Spencer, listened to the doctor's story with a grave face.

"And I think, Miss Hart," said Doctor Mendel, in conclusion, "that you would better stay in Rockwell over night, and return to the city tomorrow."

"I *don't* think so!" said Miss Hart, with such emphasis that the three men looked at her in surprise.

"If you will go home with me," said Mr. Maynard, "Mrs. Maynard will give you a warm welcome, and then you can decide to-morrow on your further plans."

"No," said Miss Hart, who seemed to be a young woman of great decision of character, "I shall go straight to Mrs. Spencer's. I am engaged to go there to-night, and I want to go. I am not at all afraid of the diphtheria, and as Delight is perfectly well, she can begin her lessons just as we planned to do. This will keep her interested and prevent her from worrying as much as if she were idle. And then, if anything should happen, I will be there to assist Mrs. Spencer."

"Thank you, Miss Hart," said Mr. Spencer, shaking her hand. "You are a noble woman, and I shall be so glad to have you there with my wife. I've been trying to think how I could get a companion for her, but none of her city friends would enter the house, nor could they be expected to. And, of course, no Rockwell neighbors can go in. But you will be a tower of strength, and I shall be immensely relieved to have you there."

Doctor Mendel was pleased too, at the turn affairs had taken, for he feared Mrs. Spencer would break down under the nervous strain, if she had to bear her trouble alone.

So when Mr. Maynard took Mr. Spencer to his own home, Doctor Mendel took Miss Hart to Mrs. Spencer's.

"I've brought you another visitor," he cried, cheerily, as he entered the quarantined house.

"Why, Doctor," said Mrs. Spencer, "you said nobody could come in!"

"No, not if they're to go out again. But Miss Hart has come to stay."

"Oh, how splendid!" cried Mrs. Spencer, "are you really willing to do so?"

"Yes, indeed," answered Miss Hart. "And it looks to me as if I should have two pupils instead of one." She looked kindly at Marjorie, who smiled in return, though she did not at all feel sure that she wanted lessons added to her other troubles.

But Miss Hart seemed to ignore the fact that there were any troubles for anybody.

She talked pleasantly, even gaily, with Mrs. Spencer. She chatted merrily with Delight and Marjorie; and she even went out and spoke very kindly to the afflicted Maggie. And it was partly due to her suggestions that Mary, who was acting as cook, added some special dainties to the menu, and sent up an unusually good dinner. The party that gathered round the table was not a sad one, but this was due to the combined efforts of Miss Hart and Marjorie.

Midget remembered her father's rules, and pretended she was just staying with the Spencers for one night. She was so fond of "pretending," that this part came easy. Then she had put out of her mind the idea that she might have the diphtheria, and moreover, she was trying really hard not to be sorry for herself. In consequence of all this, she was gay and merry, and she was helped to be so by Miss Hart, who was good cheer itself.

The new governess was a pretty little woman, with smooth dark hair, and snapping black eyes, that seemed to read people's innermost thoughts. Although not entirely unacquainted with the Spencers, she had never before lived with them, but had been governess in the family of a friend of theirs. She was anxious for this new position, and Mrs. Spencer, who had been pleased to have her come, was doubly glad to have her in this emergency.

"We won't begin to-morrow," said Miss Hart, when the subject of lessons was broached, "but I think we'll begin next day. We'll spend to-morrow getting acquainted, and learning to like each other. You'll join the class, won't you, Marjorie?"

"Yes, I think I'd like study that way," said Midge; "but I don't like school."

"I'll guarantee you'll like study in our class," said Miss Hart, smiling; "you'll be sorry when school hours are over."

Midge could hardly think this, but of one thing she was certain, that Miss Hart would be a pleasant teacher.

Soon after dinner, Marjorie's suitcase arrived.

James brought it over, and set it on the front porch and rang the bell. Then he went away before the door was opened, as he had been instructed to do.

When Marjorie opened the bag she found a note from each of the family, and they were all written in verse.

She read them aloud to the Spencer household and soon they were all laughing at the nonsense rhymes.

Her mother had written:

"Midget, Midget, Don't be in a fidget. Don't be sad and tearful, Just be gay and cheerful; Don't be sadly sighing, For the days are flying, And some day or other You'll come home to MOTHER."

"Why, that's as good as a valentine," said Miss Hart, as Midget finished reading the lines.

"So it is!" said Marjorie, smiling; "I'm going to pretend they're all valentines. Here's father's."

"Marjorie, Midget Mopsy, The world is tipsy-topsy!   When I am here And you are there I feel all wipsy-wopsy! But soon you will be home once more, And all will be as it was before; So make the most of your fortnight's stay, For I cannot spare you another day!"

By this time Delight's spirits had risen to such an extent that she exclaimed:

"I think it's splendid to have Marjorie here for two weeks!"

"We'll make a picnic of it," said Miss Hart. "You girls won't often have two weeks together, so we must cram all the pleasure into it we can."

Cramming pleasure into this dreadful time was a new idea to Delight, but she was willing to agree to it, and Marjorie said:

"I think we can be happy if we try. But we have to forget the bad parts and only remember the good."

"That's it," said Miss Hart. "Now read us another of your letters. I'm sure they're good parts."

"This one is from King,--that's Kingdon, my brother," explained Marjorie, as she took up the next note.

"Mops is a captive Princess now, She can't get out of prison; But when it's time to let her go, Oh, won't she come home whizzin'! This poetry isn't very good, But it's the best that I can sing, I would do better if I could,   And I'm your loving brother KING."

"What a jolly boy!" said Miss Hart, "I'd like to know him."

"You will," said Midget, "after our two weeks' picnic is over." She smiled at Miss Hart as she said this, accepting her idea of making a picnic of their enforced imprisonment.

"Now, here's Kitty's," she went on. "Kitty's not a very good poet, but she always wants to do what the rest do."

"Marjorie Maynard nice and sweet, Has to stay across the street. Fourteen days and fourteen nights, Visiting her friend Delight. Marjorie Maynard, nice and pretty, Come home soon to sister KITTY."

"Why, I think that's fine," said Miss Hart. "Your family are certainly devoted to you."

"Yes, they are," said Midget. "There's another,--Rosy Posy,--but she's only five. She can't write poetry."

"Can you?" asked Miss Hart.

"Yes, I can make as good verses as Kit; but not as good as King or father. We always make verses for each other on birthdays, so we get lots of practise. And we made some valentine verses this afternoon, didn't we, Delight?"

"Yes, that is, you did. But, oh, Marjorie, we can't send those valentines! Nothing like that can go out of the house!"

"Oh, pshaw, I don't believe they could do any harm."

"Well, Doctor Mendel said we mustn't send a letter of any sort, and a valentine is just the same, you know."

"What do you think, Miss Hart?" asked Marjorie.

"I'm afraid you can't send them, my dear. But we'll ask the doctor. Perhaps, if they're disinfected--"

"Oh, horrors!" cried Midget; "a valentine disinfected! Of all things! Why, it would smell of that horrid sulphur stuff instead of a sweet violet scent! Nobody would want that sort of a valentine."

"No, they wouldn't," agreed Delight. "Oh, dear, it's too bad!"

"Never mind, Delight," said Marjorie. "We can send valentines to each other, and to Miss Hart, and to your mother. Oh, yes, and to Maggie and Mary. I guess that's about all. But everybody can send them to us! That will be lots of fun! It seems selfish, doesn't it, to get lots of valentines and not send any? But it isn't selfish, because we can't help it."

"I can send to my friends in New York," said Delight, thoughtfully, "by letting father get them and send them. I can telephone him a list, you know. It isn't as much fun as if I picked them out myself, but I don't want the girls to think I've forgotten them."

"If they know about the quarantine, they won't open the valentines," suggested Marjorie; "they'll think they came from this house, and they'll be frightened."

"That's so," agreed Delight; "unless they look at the postmark and it's New York."

"Well, then, if they don't know your father's writing, they'll never know they came from you anyway."

"No, they won't. But then people never are supposed to know who sends a valentine."

"Then what's the good of sending any?"

"Oh, it always comes out afterward. I hardly ever get any that I don't find out who they're from, sooner or later."

"Nor I either. Well, we'll do the best we can."

Marjorie sighed a little, for Valentine Day was always a gay season in the Maynard home, but she had promised not to be sorry for herself, so she put the thought away from her mind.

As Mrs. Spencer's room opened into Delight's, she decided to give that to Marjorie, and take the guest room herself. She felt sorry for the child, held there by an unfortunate accident, and determined to do all she could to make her stay pleasant. And she thought, too, it would please Delight to have Marjorie in the room next her own. So when the two girls went upstairs that night, they were greatly pleased to find themselves in communicating rooms.

"We can pretend, while we're getting ready for bed," said Delight, and soon, in her little kimono, and bedroom slippers, she stalked into Midget's room and said, with despairing gestures:

"Fellow princess, our doom hath befell. We are belocked in a prison grim, and I fear me, nevermore will we be liberated."

"Say not so, Monongahela," answered Marjorie, clasping her hands. "Methinks ere morning dawns, we may yet be free."

"Nay, oh, nay! the terrible jailer, the Baron Mendel, he hast decreed that we stay be jailed for two years."

"Two years!" gasped Midget, falling in a pretended swoon. "Ere that time passes, I shall be but a giggling maniac."

"Gibbering, you mean. Aye, so shall I."

"Well, stop your gibbering for to-night," said Mrs. Spencer, who came in, laughing; "you can gibber to-morrow, if you like, but now you must go to bed. Fly, fair princess, with golden hair!"

Delight flew, and Mrs. Spencer tucked Marjorie up in bed, in an effort to make the child feel at home.

There wasn't the least resemblance between Mrs. Spencer's ways, and those of her own mother, but Marjorie was appreciative of her hostess's kind intent, and said good-night to Mrs. Spencer very lovingly. At first, there was a strong inclination to cry a little, but remembering she must not be sorry for herself, Marjorie smiled instead, and in a few moments she was smiling in her sleep. Next morning, she put on the morning dress that had come over in the suitcase, and went downstairs with Delight.

"It's just like having a sister," said Delight. "I do believe, Marjorie, I'm glad all this happened. Of course, I don't mean I'm glad Maggie's baby is so sick, but I'm glad you're staying here."

"I can't quite say that, Delight, but as I am here, I'm not going to fuss about it. There's the telephone! perhaps it's Father!"

It was Mr. Maynard, and his cheery good-morning did Marjorie's heart good.

"All serene on the Rappahannock?" he asked.

"All serene!" replied Marjorie. "The verses were fine! I was so glad to get them."

"Did you sleep well? Have you a good appetite for breakfast? Did you remember my rules? May I send you a small gift to-day? Do you think it will rain? Don't you want your kitten sent over?"

"Wait,--wait a minute," cried Marjorie. "Your questions come so fast I can't answer them,--but, yes, I would like a small gift to-day."

"Aha! I thought you'd pick out that question of all the bunch to answer. Well, you'll get it when I return from the great city. Meantime, be good and you'll be happy, and I'm proud of you, my little girl."

"Proud of me! Why?"

"Because I can tell by your voice that you're cheerful and pleasant, and that's all I ask of you. Good-bye, Mopsy, I must go for my train. The others will talk to you later on."

"Good-bye, Father, and I would like the kitten sent over."

Marjorie left the telephone with such a happy face that Miss Hart, who had just come downstairs, said:

"I'm sure you had pleasant messages from home."

"Yes, indeed," said Midget. "It was Father. He's always so merry and jolly."

"And you inherit those traits. I like fun, too. I think we shall be great friends."

"I think so too," agreed Midget, and then they all went to breakfast.

The day started auspiciously enough, but after Midge had telephoned to the rest of her family there seemed to be nothing to do. Delight had a headache, brought on probably by the excitement of the day before, and she didn't feel like playing princess.

There was no use finishing the valentines, for Doctor Mendel said they must not send them to anybody.

Miss Hart was in her own room, and the morning dragged.

Marjorie almost wished she could go to school, and she certainly wished she could go out to play. But the doctor's orders were strict against their leaving the house, so she sat down in the library to read a story-book. Delight wandered in.

"I think you might entertain me," she said; "my head aches awfully."

"Shall I read to you?" asked Midget. She had had little experience with headaches, and didn't quite know what to do for them.

"Yes, read a fairy story."

So Midget good-naturedly laid aside her own book, and read aloud to Delight until her throat was tired.

"Go on," said Delight, as she paused.

"I can't," said Midget, "for it hurts my throat."

"Oh, pshaw, what a fuss you are! I think you might read; it's the only thing that makes me forget my headache."

So Marjorie began again, and read until Delight fell asleep.

"I'm glad I kept on," thought Midget to herself; "though it did make my throat all scratchy. But I mustn't be sorry for myself, so I'm glad I was sorry for Delight. Maybe a little nap will make her head better."

CHAPTER XIII
GOLDFISH AND KITTENS

Leaving Delight asleep, Marjorie wandered out to the dining-room, where Mrs. Spencer was assisting the waitress in her duties. As Maggie was not allowed to leave the sick-room, Mary, the waitress, did the cooking, and this left many smaller offices to be performed by Mrs. Spencer.

"Can't I help you?" asked Marjorie, who was at her wits' end for occupation.

Usually, she could entertain herself for any length of time, but the strangeness of her surroundings, and a general feeling of homesickness made books or games unattractive.

"Why, no, Marjorie; little girls can't help," said Mrs. Spencer, who never thought of calling on Delight for assistance.

"Oh, yes, I can; truly I can do lots of things. Mayn't I put away that silver?"

"No; you don't know where it belongs. But if want to help me, can't you attend to Delight's canary? He hasn't had his bath, and Mary is too busy to do it. Do you know how?"

"Oh, yes; I often give our bird his bath, and clean his cage, and give him fresh seed and water. Where shall I find the birdseed?"

"In the small cupboard in Delight's playroom, the room where the bird is, you know."

"Yes'm, I know."

Marjorie ran upstairs, interested in this work, and taking the cage from its hook, set it on the table. She found the little bathtub and filled it with water of just the right warmth, and taking the upper part of the cage from its base, set it over the tub, which she had carefully placed on a large newspaper.

"There," she said, "spatter away as much as you like, while I cut a nice round paper carpet for your cage. I don't know your name, but I shall call you Buttercup, because you're so yellow."

The bird cocked his black eye at her, and seemed to approve of his new attendant, for he hopped into his bath, and splashed the water vigorously.

"You're a nice little Buttercup," went on Midget; "some bad little birdies won't jump in and bathe. There, I think that's enough; you'll wash all your feathers off! Here you go back home again."

She replaced the cage, filled the seed and water vases, and hung it back on its hook.

Midget was a capable little girl, and she took away the bathtub, and tidied up all traces of her work, as neatly as Mary could have done. Then she looked around for more worlds to conquer.

She saw the aquarium, a small round one, all of glass, in which were four goldfish.

"I think I'll give you a bath," said Midget to the fishes, laughing at the absurdity of the idea. But as she stood watching them, she observed the green mossy slime that covered the stones and shells at the bottom of the aquarium, and it occurred to her that it would be a good idea to clean them.

"There's a small scrubbing-brush in the bathroom," she said to herself, "and I can scrub them clean, and put in fresh water, and Mrs. Spencer will be so surprised and pleased."

She was about to bring a bowl of water from the bathroom to put the stones in while she scrubbed them, but she thought since there was already water in the glass, she might as well use that, and then get clean water for the fishes afterward.

"But I don't believe they'll like the soap," she thought, as, scrub-brush in hand, she was about to dip the soap in the water. "So I'll lay them aside while I scrub."

Marjorie had never had any goldfish, and knew nothing about them, so with no thought save to handle them gently, she took them out of the water, and laid them on the table in the sunlight.

She caught them by the simple process of using her handkerchief as a drag-net, and with great care, laid them softly down on the felt table-cover.

"There, fishies," she said, "don't take to your heels and run away. I'll soon clean up these dirty old stones and shells, then I'll give you nice fresh water, and put you back home again."

The stones and shells did look better, according to Midget's way of thinking, after she had vigorously scrubbed the moss from them. They shone glistening, and white, and she put them back in the aquarium and filled it with clean water, and then went for the fish.

"Ah, taking a nap, are you?" she said, as the four lay quiet on the table. But when she carefully put them back in the water, and they didn't wriggle or squirm a bit, she knew at once they were dead.

"You horrid things!" cried Midget, "what did you go and die for, just when I was fixing up your cage so nice? You're not really dead, are you? Wake up!"

She poked and pinched them to no avail.

"Oh, dear!" she sighed, "whenever I try to be good and helpful, I'm bad and troublesome. Now I must go and tell Mrs. Spencer about it. I wonder what she'll say. I wish I could tell mother first, but they'd hear me on the telephone. Perhaps the old things will come alive again. Maybe they've only fainted."

But no sign of life came from the four victims, who calmly floated on top of the water, as if scorning the clean white stones and shells below. They looked so pretty and so pathetic, that Marjorie burst into tears, and ran downstairs in search of Mrs. Spencer. That lady heard the tale with a look of mingled amusement and annoyance on her face.

"I've heard you were a mischievous child," she said, "but I didn't think you'd begin your pranks so soon."

"But it wasn't pranks, Mrs. Spencer," said Midget, earnestly. "I truly wanted to be help, fill, and I fixed the bird's cage so nicely, I thought I'd fix the fishes' cage too."

"But you must have known that fishes die out of water."

"No'm; I didn't. At least,--it seems to me now that I ought to have known it, but I didn't think about it when I took 'em out. You see, I never had any goldfish of my own."

"Well, don't worry about it, child. It can't be helped now. But I suppose Delight will feel terribly. She was so fond of her goldfish."

"I'm sure Father will let me give her some more," said Midget, "but I suppose she won't care for any others."

She went back to the library, where she had left Delight asleep, and found her just waking up.

"Delight," she said, wanting to get it over as soon as possible, "I've killed all four of your goldfish!"

"On purpose?" said Delight, still sleepy and uncomprehending.

"No, of course not. It was an accident. I just laid them on the table while I cleaned the aquarium, and they fainted away and staid fainted. I guess they must have been sick before."

"No, they weren't. They were awfully frisky yesterday. I think you're real mean, Marjorie."

"I'm awful sorry, Delight, truly I am. But I'm 'most sure Father will let me give you other fish to make up for them."

"But they won't be the same fish."

"No, of course not. But we'll get prettier ones."

"Oh, no, you needn't get any fish at all. I'd rather have a kitten."

"Oh, I can get you a kitten easily enough. James always knows where to get them. What color do you want?"

"Gray; Maltese, you know. Will he get it to-day?"

"I'll ask Mother to ask him to-day. He'll get it soon, I know."

"All right; I'd heaps rather have that than fish. I'm tired of goldfish, anyway. You can't cuddle them like you can kittens. And I never had a kitten."

"You didn't! Why, Delight Spencer! I never heard of a girl that had ***never*** had a kitten! I'll ask Mother to see about it right away. Do you want two?"

"Yes, as many as I can have. I ought to have four to make up for those goldfish."

"You can have four, if your mother'll let you," said Midget. "Ask her."

"Oh, she'll let me. She never says no to anything I want. Does your mother?"

"Yes, often. But then, I want such crazy things."

"So do I. But I get them. Go on and see about the kittens."

So Midget went to the telephone and told her mother the whole story about the goldfish.

Mrs. Maynard was surprised at Marjorie's ignorance of fish's habits, but she didn't scold.

"I do think," she said "that you should have known better; but of course I know you didn't intend to harm the fish. And anyway we won't discuss it over the telephone. I'll wait until we're together again."

"You'll have to keep a list of all my mischief, Mother," said Midget, cheerfully; "and do up the scolding and punishing all at once, when I get home."

"Yes, but don't get into mischief while you're over there. Do try, Marjorie, to behave yourself."

"I will, Mother, but I'm so tired of staying here I don't know what to do. Delight heard me say that, but I can't help it. I expect she's tired of having me here."

"I am not!" declared Delight; "now ask her about the kittens."

So Marjorie asked her mother about the kittens, and Mrs. Maynard promised to ask James to see if he couldn't find some that would be glad of a good home.

And so anxious was James to please his dear Miss Marjorie, and so numerous were kittens among James' circle of personal acquaintances, that that very afternoon, a basket was set on the Spencer's porch and the door bell was rung.

Mary opened the door and saw the basket, well-covered over.

"The saints preserve us!" she cried; "sure, it's a baby!"

She brought the basket in, and Mrs. Spencer turned back the folded blanket, and disclosed four roly-poly kittens all cuddled into one heap of fur.

"Oh!" cried Delight, "did you ever see anything so lovely! Midget, I'm *so* glad you killed the goldfish! These are a million times nicer."

"But you could have had these too," said Marjorie; "and anyway, I'll probably put these in the aquarium and drown them, by mistake!"

"Indeed you won't!" said Delight, cuddling the little balls of fur. "Oh, Mother, aren't they *dear?*"

"They are very cunning," answered Mrs. Spencer, "and I'm glad you have them. Though four seems a good many. Don't you want to give them some milk?"

"Oh, yes; and we'll teach them all to eat from one saucer, so they'll be loving and affectionate."

The kittens showed no desire to be other than affectionate, and amicably lapped up milk from the same saucer, without dispute.

There was one white, one Maltese, one black, and one yellow, and Marjorie felt sure James had chosen the prettiest he could find.

"Now to name them," said Delight. "Let's choose lovely names. You'll help us, won't you, Miss Hart?"

"You ought to call the white one Pop Corn," said Miss Hart, "for it's just like a big kernel of freshly popped corn."

"I will," said Delight, "for it's like that; but as that's a hard name to say, I'll call her Poppy for short. A white poppy, you know. Now the black one?"

"Blackberry," suggested Marjorie, and that was the chosen name. The yellow one was named Goldenrod, and the gray one Silverbell, and the four together made as pretty a picture as you could imagine. The girls spent an hour or more playing with them and watching their funny antics, and then Miss Hart proposed that they, crochet balls of different color for each little cat.

Mrs. Spencer provided a box of worsted and they chose the colors.

A red ball was to be made for Blackberry, and a light blue one for Poppy. Goldenrod was to have a yellow one, and Silverbell a pink one.

Miss Hart showed the girls how to crochet a round cover, hooping it to form a ball, and then stuffing it tightly with worsted just before finishing it.

They made the four balls and tried to teach the kittens to remember their own colors. But in this they were not very successful, as the kittens liked the balls so much they played with any one they could catch.

When Mr. Maynard came home, true to his word, he sent Marjorie a gift.

The bell rang, and there on the doorstep lay a parcel.

It proved to contain two picture puzzles.

"Oh, goody!" cried Midget. "These are just what I wanted. I've heard about them, but I've never had any, and Father told me last week he'd get me one. One's for you, Delight, and one's for me. Which do you choose?"

"Left hand," said Delight, as Marjorie's hands went behind her.

"All right; here it is."

"But I don't know how to do puzzles. I never saw one like this."

"If you knew how to do it, it wouldn't be a puzzle. I don't know either; but we'll learn."

"I'll show you how to begin," said Miss Hart. "Wait a minute."

She went out to the dining-room, and returned with two trays, oblong, square-cornered and of fairly good size.

"Make your puzzles on these," she said, "and then you can carry them around while working on them, if you want to. You can't do that, if you make them right on the table."

So with the trays on the table in front of them the girls began. Each puzzle had about a hundred and fifty pieces, and they were not easy ones. Miss Hart showed them how to find pieces that fitted each other; but would not help them after the first two or three bits were joined, for she said the fun was in doing it themselves.

"But I can't!" said Midge, looking perfectly hopeless; "these pieces are all brownish and greenish and I don't know what they are."

"I see," said Delight, her eyes sparkling; "you must find a face, or something that you can tell what it is, and start from that."

"But there isn't any face here," said Midget; "here's one eye,--if it *is* an eye!"

"Begin with that," advised Miss Hart. "Find some more of a face to go with it."

"Oh, yes; here's a nose and lips! Why, it just fits in!"

Soon the two children were absorbed in the fascinating work. It was a novelty, and it happened to appeal to both of them.

"Don't look at each other's picture," warned Miss Hart, "and then, when both are done, you can exchange and do each other's. It's no fun if you see the picture before you try to make it."

"Some pieces of mine must be missing," declared Marjorie; "there's no piece at all to go into this long, narrow curving space."

Miss Hart smiled, for she had had experience in this pastime.

"Everybody thinks pieces are lost at some stage of the work," she said; "never mind that space, Marjorie, keep on with the other parts."

"Oh!" cried Delight. "I can see part of the picture now! It's going to be a--"

"Don't tell!" interrupted Miss Hart; "after you've each done both of them, you can look at the finished pictures together. But now, keep it secret what the pictures are about."

So the work went on, and now and then a chuckle of pleasure or an exclamation of impatience would tell of the varying fortunes of the workers.

"Oh!" cried Delight. "I just touched a piece to straighten it, and I joggled the whole thing out of place!"

Then Miss Hart showed them how to take a ruler and straighten the edges,--if the edges were built; and how to crowd a corner down into a corner of the tray, and so keep the pieces in place. So engrossed were the two that Mrs. Spencer had difficulty to persuade them to come to dinner.

"Oh, Mother," cried Delight, "do wait till I find this lady's other arm. I'm sure I saw it a moment ago."

And Marjorie lingered, looking for a long triangle with a notch in the end.

But at last they set their trays carefully away, at different ends of the room, and even laid newspapers over them, so they shouldn't see each other's puzzle.

"That's the most fun of any game I ever played," said Delight, as she took her seat at the table.

"I think so too," said Midge; "are there many of them made, Miss Hart?"

"Thousands, my dear. And all, or nearly all, different."

"When we finish these," said Delight, "I'll ask my father to bring us some more. I just love to do them."

"You musn't do too many," said Miss Hart; "that stooping position is not good for little girls if kept up too long at a time."

"It did make the back of my neck ache," said Delight; "but I don't mind, it's such fun to see the picture come."

CHAPTER XIV
A PLEASANT SCHOOL

The next day lessons began. Miss Hart and Mrs. Spencer agreed that it would be better for the two little girls to have regular school hours, and Delight was glad to have Marjorie at her lessons with her.

Midge herself was not overpleased at the prospect, but her parents had approved of the plan, and had sent over her school-books.

The play-room was used as a school-room, and a pleasant enough room it was.

When the girls went in, at nine o'clock, it didn't seem a bit like school.

Miss Hart, in a pretty light house-dress, sat in a low rocker by the window. There was nothing suggesting a desk, and on a near-by table were a few books and a big bowl of flowers.

The girls sat where they chose, on the couch or in chairs, and as Midget told her mother afterward, it seemed more like a children's party than school.

"First, let's read a story," said Miss Hart, and Marjorie's eyes opened wider than ever.

"Aren't we going to have school to-day?" she asked.

"Yes, Marjorie; this is school. Here are your books,--we'll each have one."

She gave them each a copy of a pretty looking book, and asked them to open it at a certain page.

Then Miss Hart read aloud a few pages, and the girls followed her in their own books. Then she asked Delight to read, and as she did so, Miss Hart stopped her occasionally to advise her about her manner of reading. But she did this so pleasantly and conversationally that it didn't seem at all like a reading-lesson, although that's really what it was.

Marjorie's turn came next, and by this time she had become so interested in the story, that she began at once, and read so fast, that she went helter-skelter, fairly tumbling over herself in her haste.

"Wait, Marjorie, wait!" cried Miss Hart, laughing at her. "The end of the story will keep; it isn't going to run away. Don't try so hard to catch it!"

Marjorie smiled herself, as she slowed down, and tried to read more as she should.

But Miss Hart had to correct her many times, for Midget was not a good reader, and did not do nearly so well as Delight.

And though Miss Hart's corrections were pleasantly and gently made, she was quite firm about them, and insisted that Marjorie should modulate her voice, and pronounce her words just as she was told.

"What a fine story!" exclaimed Delight, as they finished it.

"Oh, isn't it great!" exclaimed Marjorie; "do you call this book a 'Reader,' Miss Hart?"

"Yes, I call it a Reader. But then I call any book a Reader that I choose to have my pupils read from. This book is named 'Children's Stories From English Literature,' so you see, by using it, we study literature and learn to read at the same time. The one we read to-day, 'The Story of Robin Hood,' is a story you ought to know well, and we will read other versions of it some day. Now, we will talk about it a little."

And then they had a delightful talk about the story they had read, and Miss Hart told them many interesting things concerning it, and the children asked questions; and then Miss Hart had them read certain portions of the story again, and this time she said Marjorie read much better.

"For I understand now," said Midge, "what I'm reading about. And, oh, Miss Hart, I'm crazy to tell King all about it! He'll just love to play Robin Hood!"

"Yes," said Miss Hart, "it makes a fine game for out-of-doors. Perhaps some day we'll find a story that we can play indoors, while you poor prisoners are kept captive."

Marjorie gave a little sigh of pleasure. If this was school, it was a very nice kind of school indeed, but she supposed that arithmetic and spelling and all those horrid things were yet to come. And sure enough, Miss Hart's next words brought sorrow to her soul.

"Now, girlies, we'll just have a little fun with arithmetic. I happen to know you both hate it so perhaps if you each hold a kitten in your arm it will cheer your drooping spirits a little."

Marjorie laughed outright at this. Kittens in school were funny indeed!

"Yes," said Miss Hart, laughing with Marjorie, "it's like Mary's little lamb, you know. I never forgave Mary's teacher for turning him out I think kittens in school are lovely. I'll hold one myself."

Then the girls drew nearer to Miss Hart, who had a large pad of paper and a pencil but no book.

And how she did it Marjorie never knew, but she made an example in Partial Payments so interesting, and so clear, that the girls not only understood it, but thought it fun.

Miss Hart said she was Mr. White, and the two children were Mr. Brown and Mr. Green, who each owed her the same sum of money. It was to be paid in partial payments, and the sharp and business-like Mr. White insisted on proper payments and exact interest from the other two gentlemen, who vied with each other to tell first how much was due Mr. White. There was some laughing at first, but the fun changed to earnest, and even the kittens were forgotten while the important debts were being paid.

"Good-bye, arithmetic!" cried Miss Hart, as the problem entirely finished, and thoroughly understood, she tossed the papers aside; "good-bye for to-day! Now, for something pleasanter."

"But that was pleasant, Miss Hart," said Marjorie; "I didn't think arithmetic could *ever* be pleasant, but it was. How did you make it so?"

"Because I had such pleasant little pupils, I think," said Miss Hart, smiling. "Now for a few calisthenics with open windows."

The windows were flung up, and under Miss Hart's leadership they went through a short gymnastic drill.

"Doesn't that make you feel good?" said Marjorie, all aglow with the exercise, as they closed the windows, and sat down again.

"That's no sort of a drill, really," said Miss Hart; "but it will do for to-day. When we get fairly started, we'll have gymnastics that will be a lot more fun than that. But now for our botany lesson."

"Botany!" cried Midge; "I've never studied that!"

"Nor I," said Delight, "and I haven't any book."

"Here's the book," said Miss Hart, taking a large white daisy from the bowl of flowers on the table.

"How many leaves has it?"

The girls guessed at the number of petals, but neither guessed right. Then they sat down in front of Miss Hart, and she told them all about the pretty blossom.

She broke it apart, telling them the names of petals, sepals, corolla and all the various tiny parts.

The two children looked and listened breathlessly. They could scarcely believe the yellow centre was itself made up of tiny flowers.

It was all so interesting and so wonderful, and, too, so new to them both.

"Is *that* botany?" said Marjorie, with wide-open eyes.

"Yes; that's my idea of teaching botany. Text-books are so dry and dull, I think."

"So do I," said Midge; "I looked in a botany book once, and it was awful poky. Tell us more, Miss Hart."

"Not to-day, dearie; it's one o'clock, and school is over for to-day."

"One o'clock!" both girls exclaimed at once; "it *can't* be!"

But it was, and as they scampered away to make themselves tidy for luncheon, Marjorie said: "Oh! isn't she lovely! Do you always have a governess like that, Delight?"

"No, indeed! My last one was strict and stern, and just heard my lessons out of books. And if I missed a word she scolded fearfully."

"I never saw anybody like Miss Hart! why that kind of school is play"

"Yes, I think so too. And it's lovely to have you here. It's so much more interesting than to have my lessons alone."

"Oh, Miss Hart would make it interesting for anybody, alone or not. But I'll be here for two weeks, I suppose. I don't mind it so much if we have school like that every day."

"And picture puzzles every evening."

"Yes, and kittens all day long!" Marjorie picked up two or three of the furry little balls, that were always under foot, and squeezed them.

At luncheon they gave Mrs. Spencer such a glowing account of their "school" that Miss Hart was quite overcome by their praise.

"It's all because they're such attentive pupils," she said modestly.

"No, it isn't," said Mrs. Spencer. "I knew what a kind and tactful teacher you were before you came. A little bird told me."

"Now how did the bird know that?" said Miss Hart, smiling, and Midget wondered if Miss Hart thought Mrs. Spencer meant a real bird.

Afternoons the governess always had to herself. If she chose to be with the family, she might, but she was not called upon for any duties. So after Midget and Delight had finished their picture puzzles, and had exchanged, and done each other's, time again seemed to hang heavily on their hands.

It was really because they felt imprisoned, rather than any real restraint. Marjorie wanted to run out of doors and play, and Delight didn't know exactly what she did want.

They were allowed to walk on the side piazza, if they chose, but walking up and down a short porch was no fun, and so they fidgeted.

"Let's get up a good, big rousing game," said Midget, "a new one."

"All right," said Delight, "let's."

"Can we go all over the house?"

"Yes, all except the attic and kitchen."

The sick child and his mother had been put in two rooms in the third story. These were shut off from the main part of the house, and were further protected by sheets sprinkled with carbolic acid which hung over them.

The children had been warned to keep as far as possible from these quarters, but the front of the house was at their disposal.

"Let me see," said Midget, who was doing some hard thinking. "I guess we'll play 'Tourists.'"

"How do you play it?"

"I don't know yet. I'm just making it up. We're the tourists, you know; and the house, the whole house in an ocean steamer. First, we must get our wraps and rugs."

Diligent search made havoc in Mrs. Spencer's cupboards, but resulted in a fine array of luggage.

The girls dressed themselves up in Mrs. Spencer's long cats, and Mr. Spencer's caps, tied on with motor-veils, made what they agreed was a fine tourist costume.

In shawl straps they packed afghans, pillows, and such odds and ends as books and pictures, and they filled travellings bags with anything they could find.

Loaded down with their luggage, they went down in the front hall, where Marjorie said the game must begin.

"Have you ever been on an ocean steamer, Delight?" she asked.

"No; have you?"

"Yes. I haven't sailed on one, you know, but I went on board to see Aunt Margaret sail. So I know how they are. This house isn't built just right; we'll have to pretend a lot. But never mind that."

"No, I don't mind. Now are we getting on board?"

"Yes, here's the gang plank. Now we go upstairs to the main saloon and decks. Be careful, the ship is pitching fearfully!"

Oblivious to the fact that steamers don't usually pitch fearfully while in port, the two travellers staggered up the staircase, tumbling violently from side to side.

"Oh, one of my children has fallen overboard!" cried Delight, as she purposely dropped Goldenrod over the banister.

"Man overboard!" cried Marjorie, promptly. "A thousand dollars reward! Who can save the precious child?" Swiftly changing from a tourist to a common sailor, Marjorie plunged into the waves, and swam after the fast-disappearing Goldenrod. She caught the kitten by its tail, as it was creeping under a sofa, and triumphantly brought it back to the weeping mother.

"Bless you, good man!" cried Delight, her face buried in her handkerchief. "I will reward you with a thousand golden ducats."

"I ask no reward, ma'am; 'twas but my humble duty."

"Say not so! You have rendered me a service untold by gold."

Delight's diction often became a little uncertain, but if it sounded well, that was no matter.

"My cabin is forty-two," said Marjorie, who was once more a tourist, on her way upstairs.

"Here is a steward," said Delight, "he will show us the way."

The steward was invisible, but either of the girls spoke in his voice, as occasion demanded.

"This way, madam," said Midget, as she led Delight to the door of her own room. "This is your stateroom, and I hope it will suit you."

"Is it an outside one?" asked Delight, who had travelled on night boats, though not across the ocean.

"Yes, ma'am. Outside and inside both. Where is your steamer trunk?"

"It will be sent up, I suppose."

"Yes, ma'am. Very good, ma'am. Now, you can be steward to me, Delight."

"Shure. This way, mum. It's Oirish, I am, but me heart is warrum. Shall I carry the baby for ye?"

"Yes," said Midget, giggling at Delight's Irish brogue, which was always funny; "but be careful. The child isn't well." The child was Blackberry, who was dressed in large white muffler of Mrs. Spencer's pinned 'round its neck.

"The saints presarve us, mum! Ye've got the wrong baby! This is a black one, mum!"

"That's all right," said Midget "She's only wearing a black veil, to,--to keep off the cold air."

"Yis, mum. Now, here's yer stateroom, mum, and 'tis the captain's own. He do be givin' it to you, 'cause ye'r such a foine lady."

"Yes, I am;" said Marjorie, complacently. "I'm Lady Daffodil of--of Bombay."

"Ye look it! And now if ye'll excuse me, mum, I'll go and get the other passengers to rights."

Delight slipped back to her stateroom, and returned with Goldenrod in her arms. She met Marjorie in the hall.

"I think I have met you before," she said, bowing politely.

"Yes," said Marjorie, in a haughty voice, "we met at the Earl's ball. I am Lady Daffodil."

"Ah, yes, I remember you now. I am the Countess of Heliotrope."

"My dear Countess! I'm so glad to see you again. Are you going across?"

"Why, yes, I think I will."

"I think you'll have to, as the ship has already started. Let us go out on deck."

As they were well bundled up, they opened the door and stepped out on the second story balcony. It was not unlike a deck, and they went and stood by the railing.

"The sea is very blue, isn't it?" said Lady Daffodil, looking down at the bare ground with patches of snow here and there.

"Yes, and see the white caps. Oh, we shall have a fine sail. Are you ever sea-sick?"

"No; never! Are you?"

"No; I have crossed eighty-seven times, so I'm used to it. Did you know there's a case of diphtheria on board?"

"No, is that so?"

"Yes. Somebody in the steerage, I believe. That's why we're stopped at Quarantine."

This struck both girls so funny that they had to stop and giggle at it.

"My precious Goldenrod!" cried the Countess of Heliotrope, "I fear she will catch it!"

"You'd better have her vaccinated at once. It's a sure cure."

"I will. But let us go inside, the sea-breeze is too strong out here."

The game seemed full of possibilities, and the tourists were still playing it when dinner time came.

So they pretended it was the ship's dining-saloon to which they went, and Mrs. Spencer and Miss Hart were strangers, passengers whom they had not yet met.

The game once explained to Miss Hart, she grasped it at once, and played her part to perfection.

"I should think," she said, finally, "that some such game as this would be a fine way to study geography!"

"Now what can she mean by that?" thought Marjorie.

CHAPTER XV
A SEA TRIP

As the days went by, Marjorie became more accustomed to her new surroundings, and felt quite at home in the Spencer household.

The baby's illness ran its course and though the child was very sick, the doctor felt hopeful that they could keep the other children free from infection. Mrs. Spencer felt keenly the trying situation, but Miss Hart was so bright and cheerful that she made everybody feel happy.

So, as far as the two little girls were concerned, it was just as if Marjorie were merely making a visit to Delight.

The children were becoming very much attached to each other. Delight greatly admired Marjorie's enthusiastic, go-ahead ways, and Midget was impressed by Delight's quiet way of accomplishing things.

Both were clever, capable children, and could usually do whatever they set out to, but Marjorie went at it with a rush and a whirl, while Delight was more slow and sure.

But Delight was of a selfish disposition, and this was very foreign to Marjorie's wide generosity of spirit. However, she concluded it must be because Delight was an only child, and had no brothers or sisters to consider.

Marjorie's own brother and sister were very attentive to their exiled one. A dozen times a day King or Kitty would telephone the latest news from school or home, and very frequently James would cross the street with a note or a book or a funny picture for Midget, from some of the Maynards. So the days didn't drag; and as for the morning hours, they were the best of all.

"It's like a party every day," said Marjorie to her mother, over the telephone. "Miss Hart is so lovely, and not a bit like a school-teacher. We never have regular times for any lesson. She just picks out whatever lesson she wants to, and we have that. Last night we bundled up and went out on the upper balcony and studied astronomy. She showed us Orion, and lots of other constitutions, or whatever you call them. Of course we don't have school evenings, but that was sort of extra. Oh, Mother, she is just lovely!"

"I'm so glad, my Midget, that you're enjoying your lessons. Do you practice every day?"

"Yes, Mother; an hour every afternoon. Miss Hart helps me a little with that, too, and Delight and I are learning a duet."

"That's fine! And you don't get into mischief?"

"No,--at least not much. I shut one of the kittens up in a bureau drawer and forgot her; but Miss Hart found her before she got very dead, and she livened her up again. So, that's all right."

"Not quite all right; but I'm sure you won't do it again. I can't seem to scold you when you're away from me, so *do* try to be a good girl, won't you, my Midget."

"Yes, Mother, I truly will."

And she did. Partly because of the restraint of visiting, and partly by her own endeavors, Marjorie was, on the whole, as well-behaved a child as any one could wish. And if she taught Delight more energetic and noisy games than she had ever heard before, they really were beneficial to the too quiet little girl.

One day they discovered what Miss Hart meant by using their steamer game for geography lessons. During school hours she proposed that they all play the steamer game.

Very willingly the girls arrayed themselves in wraps and caps, Miss Hart also wearing tourist garb, and with shawl straps and bundles, and with the kittens, also well wrapped up, they boarded the steamer.

Miss Hart, who pretended to be a stranger with whom they became acquainted on board, told them they were taking the Mediterranean trip to Naples.

The school-room was, of course, the principal saloon of the boat, and as the passengers sat round a table, Miss Hart, by means of a real steamer chart, showed them the course they were taking across the Atlantic.

Time of course was not real, and soon they had to pretend they had been at sea for a week or more.

Then Miss Hart said they were nearing the Azores and would stop there for a short time.

So they left the steamer, in imagination, and Miss Hart described to them the beauties and attractions of these islands. She had photographs and post cards, and pressed blossoms of the marvellous flowers that grow there. So graphic were her descriptions that the girls almost felt they had really been there.

"To-morrow," she said, as they returned to the ship, "we shall reach Gibraltar. There we will get off and stay several hours, and I'm sure you will enjoy it."

And enjoy it they certainly did. Next day it occurred, and when they left the ship to visit Gibraltar, they were taken to Miss Hart's own room, which she had previously arranged for them.

Here they found pictures of all the interesting points in or near Gibraltar. There were views of the great rock, and Miss Hart told them the history of the old town, afterward questioning them about it, to be sure they remembered. That was always part of her queer teaching, to question afterward, but it was easy to remember things so pleasantly taught.

She showed them pieces of beautiful Maltese lace, explaining how it was made, and why it was sold at Gibraltar, and she showed them pictures of the Moors in their strange garb, and told of their history. The luncheon bell sent them scurrying to the ship's dining-room, and they begged of Miss Hart that they might go on to Naples next day.

But she said that geography mustn't monopolize all the days, and next day, although she wasn't sure, probably there would be a session with Mr. Arithmetic.

"I don't care," said Midget, happily, "I know we'll have a lovely time, even if it *is* arithmetic."

Valentine's Day came before the quarantine was raised.

Marjorie was very sorry for this, for the doctor had said that after a few days more she could go home, and it seemed as if she might have gone for the fourteenth.

But he would not allow it, so there was nothing to do but make the best of it.

The night before Valentine's Day, however, she did feel a bit blue, as she thought of King and Kitty and even Rosy Posy addressing their valentines, and making a frolic of it as they always did.

And she thought of her father, who was always ready to help on such occasions, making verses, and printing them in his fine, neat handwriting. Of course, they would send some to her,--she knew that,--but she was losing all the jolly family fun, and it seemed a pity.

And then the telephone rang, and it was her father calling for her.

"Hello, Midget," came his cheery voice over the wire; "now I wonder if a little girl about you? size isn't feeling sorry for herself this evening."

"I'm afraid I am, Father, but I'm trying not to."

"Good for you, Sister! Now don't bother to do it, for I can tell you I'm feeling *so* sorry for you that it's unnecessary for anybody else to do that same. Now I'll tell you something to chirk you up. I suppose you have lessons to-morrow morning?"

"Yes; Miss Hart said we could have a holiday if we chose, but we didn't choose. So we're going to have special valentiney lessons,--I don't know what they'll be."

"All right; and in the afternoon, I shall send you over a valentine party. No people, you know, they're not allowed; but all the rest of a nice valentine party."

"Why, Father, how can we have a party without people?"

"Easily enough. I'll attend to that. Goodnight, now, Midget. Hop to bed, and dream hearts and darts and loves and doves and roses and posies and all such things."

"All right, I will. Good-night, Father dear. Is Mother there?"

"Yes,--hold the wire."

So Mrs. Maynard came and said a loving goodnight to her near yet faraway daughter, and Marjorie went to bed all cheered up, instead of lonely and despondent.

St. Valentine's Day was a fine, crisp winter day, with sunshine dancing on the snow, and blue sky beaming down on the bare branches of the trees.

The fun began at breakfast-time, when everybody found valentines at their plates,--for as Midge and Delight agreed, they had made so many, and they must use them up somehow. So Miss Hart and Mrs. Spencer received several in the course of the day; two were surreptitiously stuffed into Doctor Mendel's coat pockets, and the kittens each received some.

Lessons that morning were not really lessons at all. Miss Hart called it a Literature Class.

First she told the girls about the origin of Valentines, and how they happened to be named for St. Valentine, and why he was chosen as the patron saint of love. Then she read them some celebrated valentines written by great poets, and the girls had to read them after her, with great care as to their elocution.

She showed them some curious valentines, whose initials spelled names or words, and were called acrostics, and told of some quaint old-fashioned valentines that had been sent to her grandmother.

"And now," she said finally, "we've had enough of the sentimental side, I will read you a funny valentine story."

So, in her whimsical, dramatic fashion, she read the tragic tale of Mr. Todgers and Miss Tee.

"In the town of Slocum Pocum, eighteen-seventy A.D., Lived Mr. Thomas Todgers and Miss Thomasina Tee; The lady blithely owned to forty-something in the shade, While Todgers, chuckling, called himself a rusty-eating blade, And on the village green they lived in two adjacent cots. Adorned with green Venetians and vermilion flower pots.

"No doubt you've heard it stated--'tis an aphorism trite-- That people who live neighborly in daily sound and sight Of each other's personality, habitually grow To look alike, and think alike, and act alike, and so Did Mr. Thomas Todgers and Miss Thomasina Tee, In the town of Slocum Pocum, eighteen-seventy A.D.

"Now Todgers always breakfasted at twenty-five to eight, At seven-thirty-five Miss Tee poured out her chocolate; And Todgers at nine-thirty yawned 'Lights out! I'll go to bed.' At half-past nine Miss Tee 'retired'--a word she used instead. Their hours were identical at meals and church and chores, At weeding in the garden, or at solitaire indoors."

"'Twas the twelfth of February, so the chronicler avers; Mr. Todgers in his garden, and Miss Tee, of course, in hers; Both assiduously working, both no doubt upon their knees, Chanced to raise their eyes together; glances met--and, if you please, Ere one could say Jack Robinson! tut-tut! or fol-de-re! Thomasina loved Mr. Todgers; Mr. Todgers loved Miss Tee!

"Two heads with but a single thought went bobbing to the dust, And Todgers smiled sub rosa, and Miss Thomasina blushed; Then they seized their garden tackle and incontinently fled Down the box-edged pathways past the flower pots of red;

Past the vivid green Venetians, past the window curtains white, Into their respective dwellings, and were seen no more that night.

"All that night poor love-sick Todgers tried his new-born hopes to quell, And Miss Tee made resolutions, but she did not make them well, For they went to smash at daybreak, and she softly murmured "Tis Kismet! Fate! Predestination! If he'll have me I am his.' While Todgers sang 'There's Only One Girl in This World for Me,' Or its music hall equivalent in eighteen-seventy.

"It was February thirteenth (On, my Pegasus! Nor balk At that fear-inspiring figure!) Thomasina took a walk. And Fate drew her--drew her--drew her by a thousand spidery lines To a Slocum Pocum window filled chockful of valentines, All gaudy--save two, just alike in color, shape and size, Which pressed against the window pane and caught the lady's eyes.

"'How chaste! How charming! How complete!' she cried. 'It must be mine! I'll tell my love to Thomas in this lovely valentine, Whereon is suitably inscribed, in letters fine and free, 'SEND BACK THIS TENDER TOKEN IF YOU CANNOT MARRY ME.' So with her cheeks all rosy, and her pulses all astir, She went in and brought the valentine and took it home with her.

"Ten minutes later Thomas paused outside the self-same store. You guess the rest. Fate grappled him and pushed him through the door, And made him buy the fellow to the very valentine Which Thomasina had purchased there at twenty-five to nine. He chuckled (and Fate chuckled) the appropriate words to see-- 'SEND BACK THIS TENDER TOKEN IF YOU CANNOT MARRY ME.'

"It was February fourteenth, and the postman's rat-a-tat Made two hearts in Slocum Pocum beat a feverish pit-pat Thomas and Thomasina each in turn rushed doorwards and Snatched their respective missives from the post's extended hand; And the postman, wicked rascal, slowly winked the other eye, And said: 'Seems to me the old folks is a gettin' pretty spry.'

"They tore the letters open. 'What is this? Rejected! Spurned!' Both thought the cards before them were their valentines returned. And Thomas went to Africa, and Thomasina to Rome; And other tenants came to fill each small deserted home. So no more in Slocum Pocum may we hope again to see Poor Mr. Thomas Todgers and poor Thomasina Tee."

"That's awfully funny," said Delight, as Miss Hart finished reading, "but I should think they would have known they got each other's valentine."

"I shouldn't," said Midge, who entered more into the spirit of the story; "they didn't know each other sent any, so each thought their own was returned. Besides, if they hadn't thought so, there wouldn't have been any story."

"That's so," said Delight, who usually agreed with Marjorie, finally.

The postman brought lots of valentines for the two little girls. Delight's were almost all from her friends in New York, although some of the Rockwell young people had remembered her too.

Marjorie's were nearly all from Rockwell, and though there were none from any of her family, that did not bother her, for she knew they would come in the afternoon for the "party."

CHAPTER XVI
A VALENTINE PARTY

At four o'clock the "party" came. Midget and Delight, watching from the window, saw James and Thomas come across the street, bringing between them a great big something, all wrapped in white tissue paper. They left their burden, whatever it was, on the porch, rang the doorbell, and went away.

The children flew to the door, and, with the help of Mary and Miss Hart, they brought the big thing in.

Though bulky, it was not heavy, and they set it in the library and proceeded to take off the wrappings. As the last sheet of tissue paper was removed, shrieks of admiration went up from the girls, and Mrs. Spencer came running in to see what the excitement was about.

She saw a large heart, about five feet high, made on a light wood frame, which was covered with red crepe paper. It was bordered with red and white gilt flowers, also made of paper, and at the top was a big bow of red ribbon, with long fluttering streamers. On top of the heart, of either *shoulder*, sat two beautiful white doves which were real doves, stuffed, and they held in their beaks envelopes, one marked Delight and one Marjorie.

The whole affair had a back stay, and stood up on the floor like an easel. The paper that covered the heart was put on in folds, like tucks upside down, and in the folds were thrust many envelopes, that doubtless contained valentines. Between and among these were little cupids and doves fastened on, also nosegays of flowers and fluttering ribbons, and hearts pierced with darts, and the whole effect was like one great big valentine.

Before touching the envelopes, Delight and Marjorie sat on the floor, their arms round each other, and gazed at the pretty sight.

"Did your father make it?" asked Delight.

"He planned it, I'm sure," replied Marjorie. "But they all helped make it, I know. I suppose Father had the frame made somewhere, then he and Mother covered it, and Kit and King helped make the flowers and things. Oh, I wish I'd been there!"

"Then they wouldn't have made it!" said Delight, quickly, and Midge laughed, and said:

"No, I suppose not. Well, shall we begin to read the valentines?"

"Yes, but let's take them out slowly, and make it last a long while."

"Yes, for this is our 'party,' you know. Oh, see, these envelopes in the doves' bills say on them, 'To be opened last.' So we'll begin with these others. You take one with your name on, first."

So Delight pulled out an envelope that was addressed to her.

It contained a valentine of which the principal figure was a pretty little girl, something like Delight herself. Inside was written:

"Flossy Flouncy, fair and fine, Let me be your Valentine. Here's my heart laid at your feet, Flossy Flouncy, fair and sweet."

"I know King wrote that!" cried Midget; "he always calls you Flossy Flouncy. You don't mind, do you?"

"No, indeed! I think it's fun. I'm going to call him Old King Cole. That is, if I ever see him again."

"Oh, pshaw! We'll be out of this prison next week. The doctor said so. And you must come and make me a visit to even things up."

"Mother wouldn't let me go to your house to stay, I'm sure; but I can go over afternoons or Saturdays."

"Yes, and you'll get to know King better. He's an awful nice boy."

"I'm sure he is. Now you take a valentine."

Midget pulled out the biggest one that was addressed to her. It held a beautiful, large valentine, not home-made, but of most elaborate design.

On its back, though, was a verse written, that Midge knew at once was done by her father. It said:

"Marjorie Midget Mopsy Mops, I have looked through all the shops, Searching for a Valentine Good enough for Midget Mine. This is the best that I could do, So here it is with my love so true."

"Isn't it a beauty!" cried Midge; "I never had such a handsome one before. See how the flowers are tied with real ribbons, and the birds hop in and out of their cages."

"It's splendid!" said Delight, "and here's a big one for me too!"

She pulled out a large envelope, addressed to herself, and found a valentine quite as beautiful as Marjorie's and almost exactly like it. It was from her father, and as Mr. Spencer didn't have the knack of rhyming as well as Mr. Maynard, he had written on the back:

"Dear Delight, I can't write, But I send you Affection true, Yankee Doodle Doo!"

"I think that's funny!" cried Marjorie. "I love funny valentines."

"So do I," agreed Delight; "and I didn't know father could make rhymes as well as that. He must have learned from your father."

"I 'spect he did. Everybody makes verses at our house."

Marjorie smiled to think of the grave and dignified Mr. Spencer learning to write funny rhymes, but she was glad Delight had a big valentine like hers.

Then they pulled out the others, by turns. Some were lovely ones that had been bought; some were home-made ones; some were funny, but the funny ones were home-made, they were not the dreadful things that are called "comic" valentines.

Then there were valentines from Gladys and her brother Dick, which had been delivered by the postman at Marjorie's home, and sent over with the others. There was one from each of the home servants, who were all fond of Midget, and glad to send her a token of remembrance. And among the best of all were valentines from Grandma Sherwood and Uncle Steve.

Uncle Steve was especially clever at writing verses, and he sent several valentines to both the girls.

One bore a picture of two weeping maidens, behind barred windows in a castle tower. The verses ran thus:

"Two Princesses locked in a tower,
Alas, alas for they! I would they need not stay an hour,

Nor yet another day. But to a lovely rosy bower
The two might fly away.
"I would I were a birdie fleet
That I might wing a flight, And bear to them a message sweet
Each morning, noon and night. Twould be to me a perfect treat
To see their faces bright.
"But, no, in their far home they stay,
And I must stay in mine; But though we are so far away
Our thoughts we may entwine. And I will send this little lay

From your fond
"VALENTINE."

"That's lovely," said Delight, "and it's for me as much as you. What jolly relatives you have."

"Oh, Uncle Steve is wonderful. He can do anything. Sometime perhaps you can go to his house with me, then you'll see. Oh, here's a pretty one, listen."

Midge read aloud:

"What is a Valentine? Tell me, pray. Only a fanciful roundelay Bearing a message from one to another (This time, to a dear little girl from her mother). Message of love and affection true; This is a Valentine, I LOVE YOU!"

"That's sweet. Did your mother write it?"

"Yes, Mother makes lovely poetry. Here's a ridiculous one from Kit."

"Marjorie, Parjorie, Pudding and Pie, Hurry up home, or I'll have to cry. Since you've been gone I've grown so thin I'm nothing at all but bone and skin. So hurry up home if you have any pity For your poor little lonesome sister

"KITTY."

"Why, I thought people never signed valentines," said Delight, laughing at Kitty's effusion.

"They don't, real ones. But of course these are just nonsense ones, and anyway I know Kit's writing, so it doesn't matter."

There were lots of others, and through Marjorie, naturally, had more than Delight, yet there were plenty for both girls, and set out on two tables they made a goodly show. Miss Hart was called in to see them, but she answered that she was busy in the dining-room just then, and would come in a few moments.

The big heart that had held the valentines was not at all marred, but rather improved by their removal, and, the girls admired it more than ever.

"But we haven't taken the last ones yet," said Delight, looking at the two envelopes in the bills of the doves. They took them at the same time, and opened them simultaneously.

Each contained a valentine and a tiny parcel. The valentines were exactly alike, and their verses read the same:

"This is a Ring Dove, fair and white That brings this gift to you to-night. But why a Ring Dove, you may ask; The answer is an easy task. Look in this tiny box and see What has the Ring Dove brought to thee!"

Eagerly the girls opened the boxes, and inside, on a bit of cotton wool, lay two lovely rings exactly alike. They were set with a little heart made of tiny pearls and turquoises, and they just fitted the fingers of the two little girls.

"Aren't they exquisite!" cried Delight, who loved pretty things.

"Beautiful!" agreed Midge, who thought more of the ring as a souvenir. "We can always remember to-day by them. I suppose your father sent yours and my father sent mine."

"Yes, of course they did. Oh, Miss Hart, do look at our rings and valentines!"

Miss Hart came in, smiling, and proved an interested audience of one, as she examined all the pretty trifles.

"And now," said Miss Hart, at last, "there's more to your valentine party. Will you come out to the dining-room and see it?"

Wondering, the two girls followed Miss Hart to the dining-room, and fairly stood still in astonishment at the scene. As it was well after dusk now, the shades had been drawn, and the lights turned on. The table was set as if for a real party, and the decorations were all of pink and white.

Pink candles with pretty pink shades cast a soft light, and pink and white flowers were beautifully arranged. In the centre was a waxen cupid with gilt wings, whose outstretched hands bore two large hearts suspended by ribbons. These hearts were most elaborate satin boxes, one having Marjorie on it in gilt letters and the other Delight. As it turned out, they were to be kept as jewel boxes, or boxes for any little trinkets, but now they were filled with delicious bon-bons, the satin lining being protected by tinfoil and lace paper.

The table was laid for four, and at each place was a valentine.

Mrs. Spencer and Miss Hart took their seats, but, at first, the girls were too bewildered to understand.

"It's your party, Marjorie," said Miss Hart, smiling. "Your father and mother sent it all over,--everything, even the candles and flowers. All we've done is to arrange it on the table. So you must sit at the head, as you're hostess."

So Midget took her place at the head of the table, with Delight opposite.

Each person had a parcel at their plate, daintily tied up in pink paper and white ribbon, and sealed with little gold hearts.

Mrs. Spencer said they would not open these until after the feast, so after they had looked a few moments longer on the pretty things all about the table, Mary brought in the first course, and the party began.

First there was fruit, and this consisted of a slice of pineapple cut in a heart shape, and surrounded on the plate by strawberries and candied cherries. This dainty arrangement, on lace paper, was so pretty that Delight said it was too bad to disturb it.

"It's too good not to be disturbed," said Marjorie, and as it was really dinner time, and the girls were hungry, the lovely fruit course soon disappeared.

"This isn't dinner," said Mrs. Spencer, "it's a party supper. Your party, you know, Marjorie."

"Yes'm; I didn't see how Father could send me a party without people. But he did his part, didn't he?"

"Yes, indeed; and we're doing ours. We've all the people that we can have, and so we'll make the best of it."

"I think it's a lovely party," said Delight, "the best one I ever went to. Oh, what are these?"

For Mary was just passing the most fascinating looking dish. It was oyster croquettes, carefully moulded in heart shapes, accompanied by French fried potatoes also cut into little hearts.

"Ellen cut these, I know she did," said Marjorie. "She's such a clever cook, and she loves to make fancy things."

"Your mother is very fortunate with her servants," said Mrs. Spencer, with a little sigh.

And then came lovely brown bread sandwiches, of course they were heart shaped too, and Marjorie declared she'd have heart-disease if these things kept on!

But they did keep on. Next came jellied chicken that had been moulded in heart forms, and lettuce salad with red hearts cut from beets among the crisp yellow leaves.

Then came dessert, and it was a bewildering array of heart ice creams, and heart cakes, and heart bon-bons, and heart shaped forms of jelly.

"Only one of each, to-night," said Mrs. Spencer, smiling. "I don't want two invalids for valentines, I can assure you."

So lots of the good things were left over for next day, and Marjorie remarked that she thought the next day's feast was always about as much fun as the party any way.

"Now for our presents," said Delight, as the last plates were removed, and they sat round the table still feasting their eyes on the pretty trinkets that decorated it.

So Mrs. Spencer opened her parcel first.

She found a silver photograph frame shaped like a heart. Of course, Mr. Spencer had sent it, and the pretty card with it read:

"As at my verse I'm sure you'd sniff, I simply send this little gift.

"VALENTINE."

The Spencers seemed to think this a fine poem but Marjorie secretly wondered if a grown-up man could think those words rhymed!

Miss Hart opened her box next, and found a heart-shaped filigree gold brooch of great beauty. The Maynards had sent her this, not only as a valentine, but as a token of gratitude for her kindness to Marjorie.

These verses were written on a fancy card:

"Hearts to Miss Hart So I bring you a heart. Your name is fine For a Valentine. Though this trinket small Can't tell you all 'Twill give you a hint That hearts are not flint; And when this one of gold Our good wishes has told, May it brightly shine As your valentine."

"It's just a darling!" exclaimed Miss Hart, looking at the welcome gift. "Your parents are too good to me, Marjorie."

"I'm glad of it," said Midge, simply, "you're too good to me!"

She smiled at Miss Hart, and then she and Delight opened their boxes together.

Their gifts were just alike, and were pink and gold cups and saucers. The china and decoration were exquisite, and both cup and saucer were heart shaped. Not the most convenient shape to drink from, perhaps, but lovely for a souvenir of Valentine's Day.

Then they took the boxes held out by the wax cupid, and admired the tufted satin and the painted garlands.

"Let's take the candies out and put them in other boxes," said Delight, "so there'll be no danger of getting a bit of chocolate on the satin."

This was a good idea, and then they took all the pretty ornaments into the library and set them around on tables.

"It's like Christmas," said Delight, with a little sigh of happiness. "I do love pretty things."

"Then you ought to be happy now," said Miss Hart, "for I never saw such an array of favors."

And indeed the room looked like a valentine shop, with its flowers and gifts and cupids and valentines, and the big heart standing in front of the mantel.

Then Miss Hart spent the evening playing games with the children, and after an enthusiastic telephone conversation with the people opposite, Marjorie and Delight went upstairs, agreeing that nobody had ever had such a lovely Valentine party.

CHAPTER XVII
A JINKS AUCTION

At last the day came when Marjorie was allowed to go home. Doctor Mendel had had a most thorough fumigation and disinfection, and all danger was over. The little boy was convalescent, and there was no longer any reason why Midget or Mr. Spencer should be exiled from their homes.

And so, liberated from her prison, Midget flew, across the street, and into the arms of her waiting family.

"Mother first!" she cried, as they all crowded round, but so mixed up did the Maynards become, that it was one grand jumble of welcoming hugs and kisses.

"Oh, I'm *so* glad to be home again," Marjorie cried, as she looked about the familiar living-room. "It seems as if I'd been away years."

"Seems so to me, too," said Kitty, who had greatly missed her sister. "Mother, aren't we going to celebrate Mopsy's coming home?"

Now "celebration" in the Maynard household, always meant dress-up frocks, and ice cream for dessert.

"Of course," said Mrs. Maynard, smiling; "fly upstairs, girlies, and get into some pretty dresses, and then fly down again, for father's coming home early."

So Midge and Kitty flew, and King scampered to his room also, and Mrs. Maynard gave the baby over to Nurse Nannie for a clean frock, while she herself telephoned for the ice cream. And to the order she added cakes and candied fruits and other dainties, until it bade fair to be a celebration feast indeed.

Marjorie, delighted to be in her own room once more, chattered rapidly, as she and Kitty dressed, and tied ribbons, and hooked waists for each other.

"Delight is an awfully nice girl, Kitsie," she was saying. "I didn't like her so much at first, but as we were together so much I grew to like her better."

"Is she as nice as Gladys?"

"In some ways she is. She's more fun than Glad about playing games. She loves to play pretend, and Gladys wasn't much good at that. But, of course, I'm more fond of Glad, she's my old friend. Delight is nice for a neighbor though."

Dressed in a white serge, with pipings and bows of scarlet velvet, her cheeks glowing red with the joyous excitement of getting home, and her eyes dancing with happiness, Marjorie flew downstairs just in time to tumble into the arms of her father, who was entering the hall door.

"Why, bless my stars!" he exclaimed; "who in the world is this?"

"Your long-lost daughter!" said Midge, nestling in his big, comfortable embrace.

"No! Can it be? This great big girl! Why, how you've grown! And yet,--yes, it is! my own Marjorie Mischief Mopsy Midget Maynard! Well, I *am* glad you're back where you belong!"

"So'm I! I tell you Father Maynard, it was awful hard to stay away so long."

"I know it, girlie, and I hope it won't happen again. But you know, 'into each life some rain must fall.'"

"And I did have a good time, too," went on Midge. "Isn't it funny, Father, how you can have a good time and a bad time both at once."

"Quite comic, I should say. Now, let me get my coat off, and then we'll talk matters over."

Marjorie skipped into the living-room, and plumped herself down on the sofa. Kitty and King sat close on either side, and Rosy Posy climbed into her lap and lovingly patted her face.

The four made a pretty group, and as Mrs. Maynard came in and saw them, she said:

"Well, I'm glad my quartette is whole again; it's been broken so long."

The dinner was a celebration for fair. Aside from the delicious things to eat, everybody was so gay and glad over Marjorie's return, that all was laughter and jollity.

"How different our two families are," said Midge, thoughtfully; "here we are having such fun and frolic, and the Spencers are just having an every-day, quiet dinner."

"Aren't they glad the sickness is all over?" asked Kitty.

"Yes, of course. But they never 'celebrate.' I guess they don't know how very well. And Mrs. Spencer is very quiet. Much noise makes her head ache."

"Mr. Spencer was awful quiet, too," said King. "He hardly ever laughed all the time he was here. Except the night we wrote the valentines. Then he laughed, cause we made him write poetry and he couldn't."

"Well, they're nice people," said Midge, "but awful different from us. I'm glad I'm a Maynard!"

"I'm glad you are!" said her father.

The next day Mrs. Maynard announced her intention of going over to see Mrs. Spencer, and thanking her for her care of Marjorie.

"But it does seem funny," said Midge, "to thank her for keeping me there, when I couldn't possibly get away! But she was good to me, though really she didn't pay very much attention to me. But I s'pose that was 'cause she was so bothered about the little sick boy. But, Mother, do thank Miss Hart, too. She was lovely; and she put herself out lots of times, to make it pleasant for Delight and me. Give her plenty of thanks, will you, Mother?"

"Yes, Midget; and what about Delight?"

"Oh, yes, thank her too. She was kind and pleasant,--only,--well, it seems mean to say so,--but, Mother, she is a little selfish. I didn't mind, really; only I don't think it's quite nice to be selfish to a guest."

"Perhaps not, Mar; one; but neither is it nice to criticise your little hostess."

Marjorie flushed. "I didn't mean to, Mother," she said; "but I thought it didn't count when I'm just talking to you."

"That's right, dearie; always say anything you choose to Mother, but don't criticise Delight to anybody else."

"No, Mother, I won't," and Midge gave her mother one of her biggest "bear-hugs" and then wandered off in search of Kitty.

"What are you doing, Kit?" she said, as she found her sister sitting on the big hall settle, looking out of the window.

"Waiting for Dorothy. She's coming this afternoon, and we're going to play paper dolls."

Marjorie must have looked a little disappointed, for Kitty said:

"Say, Mops, why don't you take Delight for your friend in Glad's place? It's so nice to have a friend all your own."

"I know it is, Kit," and Midget sat down beside her sister, "but somehow it seems sort of mean to put anybody in Gladys's place."

"Oh, pshaw! it doesn't either. And when Glad is so far away, too. She doesn't even write to you, does she?"

"She sent me a valentine."

"Well, but when has she written?"

"Not for a long time. But that doesn't matter. She's my friend, and I'm not going to put anybody else in her place."

Kitty grew exasperated at this foolishness, as it seemed to her, and said:

"Well, then don't put her in Glad's place. Keep her old place empty. But take Delight as a sort of, what do you call it? Substitute friend, and let her come over here to play, same as Dorothy comes to play with me."

"I'd like to do that," said Midge. "I'm awfully glad to have Delight with me, and I know she likes me."

"Then go and telephone her now. Ask her to come over, and play."

"No, not now, 'cause mother is over there, and I'd rather wait till she comes home. Let's all play together to-day."

"All right; here comes Dorothy now."

Dorothy Adams came in, very glad to see Midget again, whom she liked almost as much as she did Kitty. She took off her things, and the girls drifted into the living-room, where King sat reading.

He had a band of red ribbon round his head, in which were stuck a dozen large turkey feathers, giving him a startling appearance.

"What's the feathers for?" asked Dorothy, looking at the boy in amazement.

"Why, you see, I'm reading one of Cooper's stories," King explained, "and I can sort of feel the Indian part of it better if I wear some feathers."

"Come on and play," said Midget; "shall we play Indians?"

"No," said Kitty, promptly, "it's too rough and tumbly when we play it in the house. Let's play a pretend game."

"Aren't we going to have the Jinks Club any more?" asked Dorothy. "We haven't had it since the Fultons went away."

"Too few of us," said King; "we four, that's all."

"We might ask Delight to belong," said Marjorie, "she can cut up jinks when she feels like it."

"All right, do;" said King, "let's have Flossy Flouncy; and I'll ask Flip Henderson, he's heaps of fun. Then we'll have six, just like we had before."

"I don't like to put people in the Fultons' place," said Marjorie, dubiously.

"Now, look here, Midge, that's silly!" said King. "We can't help it that the Fultons moved away, but that's no reason we shouldn't have anybody to play with. Let's telephone for our two new members right now, and begin the club all over again."

After a little more argument Marjorie consented, and she telephoned for Delight to come over, and then King telephoned for Frederick Henderson, better known by the more euphonious name of Flip. Both accepted, and in less than half an hour the Jinks Club was in full session. The new members had been elected by the simple process of telling them that they were members, and they gladly agreed to the rules and regulations of the somewhat informal club.

"We just cut up jinks," exclaimed Marjorie, "but they have to be good jinks, for bad jinks are mischief, and we try to keep out of that."

"It sounds lovely," said Delight; "I always wanted to belong to a club, but I never have before. Can't we cut up a jink, now?"

"You must say 'cut up jinks,' Flossy Flouncy," said King, smiling at the pretty, eager face. "You can't cut 'em by ones."

"Well, cut some, and show me how."

"I believe you think we cut 'em with scissors, like paper dolls," said Marjorie, laughing.

She was really very glad to have Delight with her again, for she had become more attached than she realised to the little girl during their fortnight together.

"Show me," repeated Delight, with an air of willingness to learn.

"All right; let's have a good one. What shall it be, Mops?"

King looked at his sister with such evident faith in her power of inventiveness, that the others all looked at her too. Marjorie looked round the room.

"I'll tell you!" she cried, as a brilliant idea came to her, "we'll play auction."

"Hooray!" cried King, grasping the plan at once. "Sell everything we can move."

"Yes," cried Mops. "Where is the auction room?"

"This end of the room is the auction room," King, indicating nearly half of the long living-room. "Now, Flip and I are auctioneers and you ladies are in reduced poverty, and have to bring your household goods to be sold."

Delight and Kitty at once saw dramatic possibilities, and flew to dress for their parts. An afghan for a shawl, and a tidy for a bonnet, contented Kitty, but on Delight's head went a fluffy lamp mat, stuck through with four or five of the turkey quills discarded from King's head-dress.

Mops and Dorothy followed this lead, and soon four poverty-stricken ladies, carrying household treasures, timidly entered the auction-room.

"What can I do for you, madam?" said King, as Delight showed him a bronze statuette.

"I have lost all my fortune, sir," responded Delight, sobbing in a way that greatly pleased her hearers; "and I fear I must sacrifice my few remaining relics of my better days."

"Ah, yes, madam. Sorry to hear of your ill luck. Just leave the statuette, ma'am, we have an auction to-morrow or next week, and we'll get what we can for it."

"It's a priceless work of art," said Delight, still loudly weeping, "and I don't want less than five thousand dollars for it."

"Five thousand dollars, madam! A mere trifle for that gem! I'll get ten thousand for you, at least!"

"Ten thousand will do nicely," said Delight, giggling at last at King's pompous air.

Then Marjorie came bringing a large frilly sofa pillow.

"This is my last pillow," she said, in quavering tones. "I shall have to sleep on a brickbat tonight; but I must have bread for my children to eat. There are seven of them, and they haven't had a mouthful for two weeks."

"Oh, that's nothing!" responded Flip, airily. "Children ought not to be fed oftener than every three weeks anyway. I hate over-fed children. It makes them so cross."

"So it does," agreed Kitty. "But my children are never cross, 'cause I feed them on honey. I've brought a bust of Dante to have sold by auction. It's a big one, you see, and ought to bring a good price."

"Yes, it will, madame, I'm sure. Haven't you anything more to leave?"

"Yes, here's an umbrella, and a waste basket, and some books. They're all valuable but I have so much treasures in my house, I don't need these."

"Hurry up," put in Dorothy, "and give me a chance. I've brought these pictures," showing some small ones she had lifted from their nails in the wall, "and also this fine inkstand. Look out and don't spill the ink Also here's a vase of flowers, flowers and all. Look out and don't spill the water."

"You seem to bring spilly things, ma'am," said King, taking the goods carefully. "But we'll sell them."

Each girl trudged back and forth a few times until most of the portable things in the room were piled up on the table and sofa at the end where the boys were, and then the auction was prepared.

The boys themselves had taken down many of the larger pictures from their hooks, and the room looked, on the whole, as if a cyclone had struck it.

"They ought to be numbered," said Flip, stepping gingerly about among the things.

"Hold on a minute! I've got it!" shouted King, and rushed upstairs at top speed.

He returned with a large calendar, two or three pairs of scissors and a paste-pot.

"Cut 'em out," he directed, giving each girl a page of the calendar.

The numbers were large, more than an inch square, and soon lots of them were cut out. These, the boys pasted on all the goods for sale, making them look like real auction goods.

"Won't it hurt the things?" asked Delight, who was not used to such high-handed performances.

"'Course not! They'll wash right off. Now the auction will begin. Now, you must be rich ladies, different ones, you know."

"Here you are!" cried King, who was auctioneer by common consent; "here you are! number 24! a fine large statuette by one of the old masters. What am I bid for this?"

"Fifty cents," said Dorothy.

"Fifty cents! Do you mean to insult me, madame! Why, some old masters sell as high as fifty dollars, I can tell you! Who will bid higher?"

"One hundred dollars!" called out Delight, and the bronze statuette was declared her property.

Then other goods were put up, and, in order to make the play progress more quickly, two auctioneers were set to work, and King and Flip were both calling their wares and the bids at once.

Naturally, the bidders grew very excited. A large picture was hotly contested, Kitty bidding against Delight, while on the other block, the big inkstand was being sold. Somehow the wire of the picture became tangled round the auctioneer's foot, he stepped back and bumped into the other auctioneer who lost his balance, and fell over, inkstand and all. The heavy inkstand fell on the picture, breaking the glass, and soaking the paper engraving with ink. Much of the ink, too, went on Flip, who grabbed for it in a vain endeavor to save the situation.

The two boys laughingly straightened themselves out of their own mix up, but their laughter ceased when they saw that real damage had been done.

"Oh, dear!" said Marjorie, "this is a bad jinks after all!"

"Never mind, Mopsy," said King, magnanimously, "it wasn't your fault. It was mine."

"No, it was mine," said Midge, "for I proposed playing auction. I might have known we'd play it too hard."

"Never mind," said Kitty, "the company didn't have anything to do with the trouble, and we mustn't make them feel bad."

"I did," said Dorothy, "I brought the inkstand to the auction. I ought to have known better."

"Never mind who's to blame," said King, "let's straighten things out. The game is over."

Good-naturedly, they all went to work, and soon had everything back in its place. The broken and spoiled picture was stood behind the sofa, face to the wall, to be confessed to mother later.

"Now we're all in shape again," said King, looking proudly about the cleared up room. "Any nice little jinks to eat, Midgie?"

"I'll ask Sarah. She'll find something."

She did, and soon a large tray of cookies and lemonade refreshed the members of the Jinks Club, after which the visiting members went home.

CHAPTER XVIII
HONEST CONFESSION

I want to own up, Mother," said King, as Mrs. Maynard came into the room, just before dinner time.

"Well, King, what have you been doing now?"

Mrs. Maynard's face expressed a humorous sort of resignation, for she was accustomed to these confessions.

"Well, you see, Mothery, we had the Jinks Club here to-day."

King's voice was very wheedlesome, and he had his arm round his mother's neck, for he well knew her affection for her only son often overcame her duty of discipline.

"And the Jinksies cut up some awful piece of mischief,--is that it?"

"Yes, Mother; but it's a truly awful one this time, and I'm the one to blame."

"No, you're not!" broke in Marjorie; "at least, not entirely. I proposed the game."

"Well," said Mrs. Maynard, "before you quarrel for the honor of this dreadful deed, suppose you tell me what it is."

For answer, King dragged the big picture out from behind the sofa, and Mrs. Maynard's smile changed to a look of real dismay.

"Oh, King!" she said; "that's your father's favorite engraving!"

"Yes'm, I know it. That's the awfullest part of it. But, Mother, it was an accident."

"Ah, yes, but an accident that ought not to have happened. It was an accident brought about by your own wrong-doing. What possessed you to take that great picture down from the wall, and *why* did you splash ink on it?"

So then all the children together told the whole story of the auction game.

"But it was lots of fun!" Marjorie wound up, with great enthusiasm. "Delight is grand to play games with. She acts just like a grown-up lady. And Flip Henderson is funny too."

"But Midget," said her mother, "I can't let you go on with this Jinks Club of yours, if you're always going to spoil things."

"No, of course not. But, Mother, I don't think it will happen again. And anyway, next time we're going to meet at Delight's."

"That doesn't help matters any, my child. I'd rather you'd spoil my things than Mrs. Spencer's,--if spoiling must be done. Well, the case is too serious for me. I'll leave the whole matter to your father,--I hear him coming up the steps now."

Soon Mr. Maynard entered the room, and found his whole family grouped round the ruined picture.

"Wowly--wow-wow!" he exclaimed. "Has there been an earthquake? For nothing else could wreck my pet picture like that!"

"No, Father," said King; "it wasn't an earthquake. I did it,--mostly. We were playing auction, and my foot got tangled up in the picture wire, and the inkstand upset, and smashed the glass, and--and I'm awful sorry."

King was too big a boy to cry, but there was a lump in his throat, as he saw his father's look of real regret at the loss of his valued picture.

"Tell me all about it, son. Was it mischief?"

"I'm afraid it was. But we took all the things in the room to play auction with, and somehow I took that down from the wall without thinking. And, of course, I didn't know it was going to get broken."

"No, King; but if you had stopped to think, you would have known that it *might* get broken?"

"Yes, sir."

"Then it would have been wiser and kinder to leave it upon the wall, out of harm's way?"

"Yes, Father; much better. I didn't think. Oh,--I know that's no excuse, but that's,--well, it's the reason."

"And a very poor reason, my boy. The worthwhile man is the man who thinks in time. Thinking afterward doesn't mend broken things,--or take out inkstains. Of course, the broken glass is a mere trifle, that could have been easily replaced. But the engraving itself is ruined by the ink."

"Couldn't it be restored?" asked King, hopefully. He was not quite certain what "restored" meant, but he knew his father had had it done to some pictures.

Mr. Maynard smiled. "No, King, a paper engraving cannot be restored. What is that number pasted on it for?"

"We numbered all the things, so as to make it like a real auction," said Marjorie.

Mr. Maynard glanced round the room.

"You rascally children!" he cried; "if you haven't stuck papers on all the vases and bric-a-brac in the room! And on this tree-calf Tennyson, as I live! Oh, my little Maynards! Did anybody ever have such a brood as you?"

Mr. Maynard dropped his head in his hands in apparent despair, but the children caught the amused note in his voice, and the twinkle in his eye, as he glanced at his wife.

"Well, here you are!" he said, as he raised his head again, "for a punishment you must get all those numbers off without injury to the things they're pasted on. This will mean much care and patience, for you must not use water on books or anything that dampness will harm. Those must be picked off in tiny bits with a sharp penknife."

"Oh, we'll do it, Father!" cried Marjorie, "and we'll be just as careful!"

"Indeed you must. You've done enough havoc already. As to the picture, King, we'll say no more about it. You're too big a boy now to be punished; so we'll look upon it as a matter between man and man. I know you appreciate how deeply I regret the loss of that picture, and I well know how sorry you feel about it yourself. The incident is closed."

Mr. Maynard held out his hand to his son, and as King grasped it he felt that his father's manly attitude in the matter was a stronger reproof and a more efficacious lesson to him than any definite punishment could be.

After dinner the three children went to work to remove the pasted numbers.

A few, which were on glass vases, or porcelain, or metal ornaments, could be removed easily by soaking with a damp cloth; but most of them were on plaster casts, or polished wood, or fine book bindings and required the greatest care in handling.

When bed-time came the task was not half finished, and Marjorie's shoulders were aching from close application to the work.

"Sorry for you, kiddies," said Mr. Maynard, as they started for bed, "but if you dance, you must pay the piper. Perhaps a few more evenings will finish the job, and then we'll forget all about it."

Mr. Maynard, though not harsh, was always firm, and the children well knew they had the work to do, and must stick patiently at it till it was finished.

"Good-night, Father," said King, "and thank you for your confidence in me. I'll try to deserve it hereafter."

"Good-night, my boy. We all have to learn by experience, and when you want my help, it's yours."

The straightforward glance that passed between father and son meant much to both, and King went off to bed, feeling that, if not quite a grown man, he was at least a child no longer in his father's estimation.

After the children had gone, Mr. Maynard picked out the most delicate or valuable of the "auction" goods, and began himself to remove the pasted numbers.

"Partly to help the kiddies," he said to his wife, "and partly because I know they'd spoil these things. It's all I can do to manage them successfully myself."

Next morning at breakfast Mrs. Maynard said; "Well, Midget, now you're at home again, what about starting back to school?"

"Oh, Mother!" said Marjorie, looking disconsolate. And then, for she did not want to be naughty about it, she added: "All right; I s'pose I must go, so I will. But as to-day's Friday I can wait till Monday, can't I?"

Mrs. Maynard smiled. "Yes, I think you may till Monday, if you want to. But are you sure you want to?"

"'Deed I *am* sure!"

"And nothing would make you want to go to-day, instead of waiting till Monday?"

"No, *ma'am*! no-thing!" and Midget actually pounded the table with her knife-handle, so emphatic was she.

"You tell her, Fred," said Mrs. Maynard, smiling at her husband.

"Well, Madcap Mopsy," said her father, "try to bear up under this new misfortune; your mother and I have planned a plan, and this is it. How would you like it, instead of going to school any more,--I mean to Miss Lawrence,--to go every day to lessons with Delight and Miss Hart?"

Marjorie sat still a minute, trying to take it in. It seemed too good to be true.

Then dropping her knife and fork, she left her chair and flew round to her father's place at table. Seeing the whirlwind coming, Mr. Maynard pushed back his own chair just in time to receive a good-sized burden of delighted humanity that threw itself round his neck and squeezed him tight.

"Oh, Father, Father, Father! do you really mean it? Not go to school any more at all! And have lessons every day with that lovely Miss Hart, and my dear Delight? Oh, Father, you're *such* a duck!"

"There, there, my child! Don't strangle me, or I'll take it all back!"

"You can't now! You've said it! Oh, I'm so glad! Can I start to-day?"

"Oho!" said Mrs. Maynard; "who was it that said *nothing* could make her want to go to-day instead of Monday?"

Marjorie giggled. "But who could have dreamed you meant this?" she cried, leaving her father and flying to caress her mother. "Oh, Mumsie, won't it be lovely! Oh, I am *so* happy!"

"If not, you're a pretty good imitation of a happy little girl," said her father; "and now if you'll return to your place and finish your breakfast, we'll call it square."

"Square it is, then," said Marjorie, skipping back to her place; "Kit, did you ever hear of anything so lovely!"

"Never," said Kitty, "for you. I'd rather go to school and be with the girls."

"I didn't mind when Gladys was here, but I've hated it ever since I was alone. But to study with Miss Hart,--oh, goody! Is she willing, Mother?"

"Of course, I've discussed it with her and with Mrs. Spencer. Indeed, Mrs. Spencer proposed the plan herself, when I was over there yesterday. She and Miss Hart think it will be good for Delight to have some one with her. So, Midge, you must be a good girl, and not teach Delight all sorts of mischief."

"Oh, yes, Mother, I'll be so good you won't know me. Can I start to-day?"

"Yes, if you're sure you want to."

"Want to? I just guess I do!" and Midget danced upstairs to dress for "school."

The plan worked admirably. Miss Hart was not only a skilled teacher, but a most tactful and clever woman, and as she really loved her two little pupils, she taught them so pleasantly that they learned without drudgery.

As the clock hands neared nine every morning, there were no more long drawn sighs from Marjorie, but smiles and cheery good-byes, as the little girl gaily left the house and skipped across the street.

The daily association, too, brought her into closer friendship with Delight, and the two girls became real chums. Their natures were so different, that they reacted favorably on one another, and under Miss Hart's gentle and wise guidance the two girls improved in every way.

It was one day in the very last part of February that Midge came home to find a letter for her on the hall table.

"From Gladys," she cried and tore it open.

"Oh, dear!" she exclaimed, "I didn't think! Miss Hart told me never to open a letter with my finger, but to wait till I could get a letter-opener. Well, it's too late now, I'll remember next time."

She looked ruefully at the untidy edges of the envelope, but pulled the letter out and began to read it.

"DEAR MARJORIE:

"I'm coming to see you, that is, if you want me to. Father has to go East, and he will leave me at your house while he goes to New York. I will get there on Friday and stay four days. I will be glad to see you again.

"Sincerely yours,

"GLADYS FULTON."

Marjorie smiled at the stiff formal letter, which was the sort Gladys always wrote, and then she went in search of her mother.

"Gladys is coming on Friday," she announced.

"That's very nice, my dear," said Mrs. Maynard; "you'll be so glad to see her again, won't you?"

"Yes," said Midget, but she said it slowly, and with a troubled look in her eyes.

"Well, what is it, dear? Tell Mother."

"I don't know exactly,--but somehow I'm not so awfully pleased to have Gladys come. You see, she may not like Delight, and I want them to like each other."

"Why do you want them to?"

"Why do I? Mother, what a funny question! Why, I want them to like each other because I like them both."

"But you don't seem anxious lest Delight won't like Gladys."

"Oh, of course she'll like her! Delight is so sweet and amiable, she'd like anybody that I like. But Gladys is,--well,--touchy."

"Which do you care more for, dearie?"

"Mothery, that's just what bothers me I'm getting to like Delight better and better. And that doesn't seem fair to Gladys, for she's my old friend, and I wouldn't be unloyal to her for anything. So you see, I don't know which I like best."

"Well, Marjorie, I'll tell you. In the first place, you mustn't take it so seriously. Friendships among children are very apt to change when one moves away and another comes. Now both these little girls are your good friends, but it stands to reason that the one you're with every day should be nearer and dearer than one who lives thousands of miles away. So I want you to enjoy Delight's friendship, and consider her your dearest friend, if you choose, without feeling that you are disloyal to Gladys."

"Could I, Mother?"

"Certainly, dear. That is all quite right. Now, when Gladys comes, for a few days, you must devote yourself especially to her, as she will be your house-guest; and if she and Delight aren't entirely congenial, then you must exclude Delight while Gladys is here. You may not like to do this, and it may not be necessary, but if it is, then devote yourself to Gladys' pleasure and preferences, because it is your duty. To be a good hostess is an important lesson for any girl or woman to learn, and you are not too young to begin."

"Shall I tell Delight I'm going to do this?"

"Not before Gladys comes. They may admire each other immensely; then there will be no occasion to mention it. When is Gladys coming?"

"On Friday. That's only three days off."

"Then we must begin to plan a little for her pleasures. As she will only be here four days, we can't do very much. Suppose we have a little party Saturday afternoon, then she can meet all her Rockwell friends."

"Yes, that will be lovely. And I do hope she and Delight will like each other."

"Why of course they will, Midget. There's no reason why they shouldn't."

CHAPTER XIX
A VISIT FROM GLADYS

Gladys came Friday afternoon and Marjorie welcomed her with open arms, truly happy to see her friend again.

"Tell me all about your new home, Glad," said Midge, as the two settled themselves on either end of the sofa for a chat.

"Oh, it's just lovely, Mops. It's like summer all the time. And the flowers are in bloom all about, and the birds sing in the trees, and everybody wears white dresses and summer hats even in February."

"That *is* lovely. And is your father getting better?"

"Yes, some better. He just *had* to come to New York on some business, but the doctor said he must not stay but a few days. So we have to start back on Tuesday."

"It's a shame. I wish you could stay longer."

"So do I. But I'm glad to go back, too. I go to a lovely school there, and I know the nicest girls and boys."

"Nicer than Rockwell children?"

"Oh, I don't know. Yes, I guess so. My most intimate friend is a lovely girl. Her name is Florence Lawton. Isn't that a pretty name?"

"Why, Gladys Fulton! I'm your most intimate friend! Do you like her better than me?"

Gladys' eyes opened wide.

"Midget Maynard," she said, "what do you mean? Of course you were my best friend here, but when I'm out there don't you s'pose I've got to have somebody else to play with and to tell secrets to?"

Somehow this idea made Midget's heart lighter. It justified her in taking Delight as a chum in Gladys' place.

"Yes, of course," she responded. "Our letters don't seem to amount to much, do they, Glad?"

"No, I'm no good at all at writing letters. Don't you have any chum in my place, Mopsy?"

"Why, yes, I s'pose I do," said Marjorie, slowly, for it was just beginning to dawn on her that Delight *had* taken Gladys' place. "I'm awfully good friends with Delight Spencer, who lives in the house you used to live in."

"Delight! what a pretty name."

"Yes, and she's an awfully pretty girl. You'll see her while you're here, of course."

Very soon the first strangeness of the reunion was over, and the two were chatting away as gaily as if they had never been separated.

Then Delight came over. She had promised Marjorie she'd come over to see Gladys, but she came rather unwillingly. The truth is, she felt a little jealous of Marjorie's older friend, and was not prepared to like her.

Delight was dressed in some of her prettiest clothes, and the big black velvet hat on her fair golden hair made a lovely picture.

Gladys thought she was beautiful, and welcomed her warmly, but Delight, when introduced, seemed to shrink back into herself and sat stiffly on the edge of a chair, holding her muff and saying nothing.

"Oh, Delight," cried Midget, "don't act like that. Take off your things, and let's play."

"No, I can't stay but a few minutes," said Delight, primly.

She sat there, looking very uncomfortable, and though Midge and Gladys tried to make her more chummy, they didn't succeed.

Finally, Delight rose to go, and as Gladys didn't care much for such a spoil sport, she said nothing to detain her. Midget went to the door with her, and as Delight went out she turned to Midge, with her eyes full of tears, and said: "You like her better than you do me, so I'll go."

"Go on, then," said Marjorie, utterly exasperated by such foolishness, as she considered it.

"What ails her?" said Gladys, as Marjorie returned.

"Why, I suppose it's because you're here. She never acted that way before. You see, she's a spoiled child, and she always wants everything her own way. It's awfully funny, Gladys, but I thought maybe you wouldn't like her and here it's the other way about!"

"Oh, I like her, or at least I would if she'd let me. I think she's the prettiest girl I ever saw. Don't you?"

"Yes, I do. And she's awfully nice, too, if she didn't have this tantrum about you."

"Oh, well, she'll get over it," returned Gladys; "I shan't be here long, anyway."

The day after Gladys' arrival was the first Saturday in March.

First Saturdays were usually "Ourdays," when Mr. Maynard took a whole day from his business and devoted it to the entertainment of his children.

It was King's turn to choose how the day should be spent, but, as a party in honor of Gladys had been arranged for the afternoon, there was only the morning to choose for.

They were all discussing the matter the night before, and King kindly offered to give his turn to one of the girls, that they might choose something to please Gladys.

"No, indeed," said Midget. "We like boys' fun as well as girls' fun; so you choose ahead, King."

"All right, then. If you girls agree, I'd like to build a snow fort. This is a jolly deep snow, the best we've had this winter, and likely the last we'll have. Father's a jim dandy at snow games, and we could have an out-of-door frolic in the morning, and then Glad's party in the house in the afternoon."

"Goody! I say yes to that," cried Midget.

"I too," said Gladys. "We don't have any snow in California, and I don't know when I'll see any again."

"I'm satisfied," said Kitty, "can I ask Dorothy over?"

"Yes," said Mr. Maynard; "ask anybody you choose."

So next morning, soon after breakfast, the children put on all the warmest wraps they could find, and in tam o'shanter caps, tippets, mittens and leggings, started out for their Ourday fun.

The snow was more than a foot deep all over the great lawn, and Mr. Maynard selected a fine place for a fort. He taught the boys,--for King had asked Flip to come over,--how to cut and pack great blocks of solid snow, and the girls he showed how to make balls and cones for decoration.

Once Midget caught sight of Delight peeping across at them from behind a curtain. "I'm going over to ask her to come," she said; "I didn't ask her before, because I thought she wouldn't come. But, I believe she will."

So Midge scampered across the street and rang the Spencer's door bell.

"Won't you come over?" she said, as soon as she saw Delight. "It's an Ourday, and we're having such fun!"

"No, thank you," said Delight; "you don't need me when you have Gladys."

"Don't be silly!" said Midget. "What's the reason I can't play with you both? Come on."

"Oh, I don't want to come," said Delight pettishly. "Go on back."

So Marjorie went back, alone, walking slowly, for she couldn't understand Delight's behavior.

But once again in the fun of the snow play, she forgot all about her ill-natured little neighbor.

They built a grand fort, with a flag waving from its summit, and then with soft snowballs for ammunition, they chose sides and had the merriest kind of a battle. Afterward they built a snow man and a snow woman.

These were of heroic size, so big that Mr. Maynard had to climb a step-ladder to put their heads in place.

The man, according to the time-honored tradition of all snow men, wore a battered old high hat, and had a pipe in his mouth, while the old woman wore a sun bonnet and checked apron.

They were comical figures, indeed, and when they were completed it was time to go in to luncheon, and Dorothy and Flip scampered for their homes.

"Now, gentlemen of the jury," said Mr. Maynard, at the lunch table, "as we have still two good hours before it's time to array ourselves in purple and fine linen for the party, suppose we continue our outdoor sports and go for a sleigh ride? It's up to you, King."

"Fine!" agreed King. "If it suits the ladies of the castle."

"It do," said Kitty; "the ladies fair would fain go for a sleigh ride. May I ask Dorothy?"

"Not this time, Kittums," said her father. "I've ordered a big double sleigh, and we'll just fill it comfortably."

And so they did, with Mr. and Mrs. Maynard on the wide back seat and Rosy Posy between, them; Midget, Gladys, and Kitty facing them, and King up on the box with the driver.

A span of big powerful horses took them flying over the snow, and the crisp, keen air made their cheeks rosy and their eyes bright.

It was a fine sleigh ride, and the jingling bells made a merry accompaniment to the children's chatter and laughter.

"Ice cream, Kitty?" asked her father as they entered a small town, and drew up before the funny little inn that was its principal hostelry--

"No, sir!" said Kitty, whose teeth were chattering, "it's too cold!"

"Well, I never expected to live long enough to hear Kitty say no to ice cream!" exclaimed Mrs. Maynard in surprise.

"It's a cold day when that happens, isn't it Kit?" asked her father. "Well, jump out then, and stamp your toes, and thaw your ears."

They all went into the little inn, and warmed themselves by the fire, and had a drink of hot milk or hot soup, as they preferred, and then bundled back into the sleigh for the homeward ride.

"I'm not cold now," said Kitty, cuddling into the fur robes.

The horses dashed back again over the snow, and soon after three o'clock they were at home.

The party was at four, so there was ample time to get ready.

"What kind of a party is it to be father?" asked Midge. "Any special kind?"

"Special kind?" said Mr. Maynard; "I should say so! It's an animal party, to be sure!"

"An animal party?" said Gladys, to Midge, as they went upstairs to dress; "what does he mean?"

"I don't know. You never can tell what Father's going to do. Especially on an Ourday. He always gets up lovely things for Ourdays."

"He's a jolly man," said Gladys; "I never saw anybody like him."

"Nor I either," agreed Midge; "I think he's just perfect."

The little girls all wore white dresses, each with a different colored ribbon, and were all ready, and sitting in state, at ten minutes before the hour appointed for the party.

"Isn't Delight coming, Mopsy?" asked Mrs. Maynard.

"No, mother; I just telephoned her, and she won't come. She's acting up foolish about Glad, you know."

"Indeed it *is* foolish," said Mrs. Maynard, looking annoyed; "I think I'll run over there and see what I can do."

"Oh, do, Mother; you always make everything come out all right."

"But I don't know whether I can make a silly little girl come out all right; however, I'll try."

Mrs. Maynard threw on some wraps and went over to the house across the street.

What arguments she used, or what she said to Delight, Marjorie never knew, but she returned, after a time, bringing both Delight and Miss Hart with her.

Delight made a beautiful picture in a filmy, lacy white frock, and a big blue bow on her golden curls.

"Hello, Flossy Flouncy!" cried King, and this broke the ice, and made it easier for Delight than a more formal greeting would have done.

"Hello, Old King Cole!" she responded, and then a number of other people came, and a general hubbub of conversation ensued.

"This is an animal party," said Mr. Maynard, when all the guests had arrived. Now where were the most animals ever gathered together?"

"In the circus!" cried one boy, and another said, "In the menagerie."

"Try again," said Mr. Maynard; "not right yet!"

"Hippodrome," shouted somebody, and "zoo!" cried somebody else, but to each Mr. Maynard shook his head.

"Go farther back," he said; "what was the first collection of animals in the world?"

And then Delight thought what he meant, and cried out, "Noah's Ark!"

"Of course!" said Mr. Maynard. "That's the place I meant. Well, then, here's an ark for each of you, and you can each play you're Noah."

He whisked a table cover off of a table by his side, and there was a great pile of toy Noah's arks. King and Flip distributed them, until everybody had one.

"Why, they're empty?" cried Midge, looking into hers.

"They won't be long," said her father. "Now, young people, scatter, and fill your arks with animals. Pretend you're hunting in the jungle, or whatever you like, but capture all the animals you can find for your arks. There are hundreds in these two rooms and the halls."

"Hidden?" asked Kitty.

"Yes, hidden and in plain sight, both. But wait; there's a schedule."

Mr. Maynard unfolded a paper, and read:

"Elephants count five, tigers ten, lions fifteen, bears five, kangaroos five, cats five; all two-legged animals or birds two, fishes one, camels twenty-five, and zebras fifty. After your arks are filled, we'll count them up according to schedule, and award prizes. Now, scoot!" They scooted, and spent a merry half hour hunting the animals. They found them in all sorts of places,--tucked in behind curtains, under sofa-pillows, between books, and round among the bric-a-brac on mantels and tables. They were the little wooden animals that belonged in the arks, and the children were greatly amused when they discovered, also, the small, queer little people that represent Noah and his family.

"I s'pose as these are two-legged animals they count as birds," said King.

"Yes," said Mr. Maynard, "all bipeds count alike."

As Marjorie made a dive for a tiger which she saw in the lower part of the hall hatrack, somebody else dived for it at the very same moment.

It was Delight, and both girls sat suddenly down on the floor, laughing at their bumped heads.

But when Delight saw that it was Midget, she stopped laughing and looked sober, and even sour.

"Don't, Delight," said Marjorie, gently, and putting her arms round her friend, she kissed her lovingly.

This melted Delight's foolish little heart, and she whispered, "Oh, Midge, you do like me best, don't you?"

But Midge was in no mood for emotional demonstration down under the hatrack, so she scrambled up, saying, "I shan't if you act as foolish as you have done. You behave decently to Gladys and to me, and then see what'll happen."

With this Midge calmly walked away and collected more animals, while Delight, rather stunned by this summary advice, jumped up and went after animals, too.

At last the collecting was over and the children brought their arks to Mr. Maynard. With Miss Hart to help him, it didn't take very long to figure out the schedule value of each ark-full, and prizes were given to those three whose score was highest.

Flip Henderson had first prize, and Delight had second, while the third went to Harry Frost. Delight was greatly pleased, and Marjorie was glad, too, for she thought it might make her more amiable.

But that wasn't the reason; the real reason was because Midge had kissed her, and then had scolded her roundly. This combination of treatment affected the strange little heart of Delight, and she began at once to be nice and pleasant to Gladys and to everybody.

The next game was like Jackstraws, but it wasn't Jackstraws.

All the ark-fulls of animals were emptied out into a heap on the table, and the children sat round. Each was given a teaspoon, and with this they must remove as many animals as possible without moving any other than the one touched. They might use either end of the teaspoon, but must not use their fingers.

The animals counted as in the former schedule and as each was picked from the pile it was given to Miss Hart, and she credited it to the player who took it.

Of course, as in Jackstraws, if one made a mis-play it was the next player's turn. This game was great fun, and they watched each other breathlessly, though careful not to joggle anybody.

"Now, Flossy Flouncy," cried King, "it's your turn. In you go! Catch a camel first thing!"

Delight was a little embarrassed at King's raillery, but she was bound she wouldn't show it, and her slim little white fingers grasped the teaspoon firmly.

She only took off a few, for the excitement of it made her nervous and her hand shook. But she was glad she didn't win a prize in that game, for nobody likes to win two prizes at the same party.

CHAPTER XX
CHESSY CATS

After that game they played several other animal games, some quiet and some noisy, and then Mr. Maynard announced that they would play "Chessy Cats."

"What in the world is that?" said Gladys to King. "I never heard of it."

"Nor I," he responded; "probably Father made it up. Well, we'll soon see."

Mr. Maynard chose two captains, one being Gladys, as it was really her party, and the other Flip Henderson.

These two captains were asked to stand opposite each other at the end of the room, and to "choose sides."

"You must each," said Mr. Maynard, "choose the girls or boys who seem to you most like Chessy Cats."

This advice was not very intelligible, but as it was Gladys' turn to choose first, she chose King.

Then Flip chose Marjorie, as it seemed to him polite to take his hostess.

Then in a burst of good feeling Gladys chose Delight, and though she wanted to refuse, she stifled her ill-nature and stood up next to King.

Then the choosing went on until all were taken, and the two long lines stood on either side of the room.

"You see," said Mr. Maynard, "this is a contest of happiness. I want to see which line of children represents the greater amount of merriment. Will you all please smile?"

Every face broke into a grin, and Mr. Maynard looked at them thoughtfully.

"You all seem happy," he said; "a fine lot of Chessy Cats. You know Chessy Cats are remarkable for their wide grins. But as I have a prize for the side that shows most grin, I have to be careful of my decision. Miss Hart, if you will help me, I think we'll have to find out **exactly** which row of Chessy Cats grins the widest."

Miss Hart, smiling like a Chessy Cat herself, came forward with a lot of short strips of white paper in her hand. She gave half of these to Mr. Maynard, and then the fun began.

They actually measured each child's grin, marking on the paper with a pencil the exact length of each mouth from corner to corner as it was stretched in a smile. Of course a fresh paper was used for each, and wide indeed was the grin when the grinner realized the absurdity of having his smile measured!

Then, of course, each tried to grin his very widest, for the success of his line and the glory of his captain. Delight's little rosebud mouth couldn't make a very wide grin, but she stretched it as wide as possible, showing her pretty white teeth, and held it motionless while it was measured.

It was astonishing how wide some of them could stretch their smiling mouths, and how absurd they looked while standing stock still to be measured. Their ridiculous grimaces caused shouts of laughter from the Chessy Cats who were not being measured at the moment.

"Midget! she's the one that counts!" cried King. "She's got a smile like an earthquake! Flossy Flouncy, here, she won't count half as much!"

Marjorie only laughed at King's comment, and spread her rosy lips in a desperate effort to beat the record.

At last all were measured, and taking a pair of scissors, Miss Hart clipped the ends off the papers where the mark was, and thus each paper represented the exact width of a smile.

The papers of each side were then placed end to end, and the whole length measured. The result was fifty-four inches of smile for Flip's side, and fifty-two for Gladys'.

"Hooray, Mopsy!" cried King. "I knew your mouth was two inches bigger than Delight's!"

"Oh, no, brother," rejoined Midge, "it's because your mouth is so tiny you can't smile very well!"

But whatever the reason, there was a good two inches difference in the aggregate, so Flip Henderson's side was the winner.

"As all the Chessy Cats grinned nobly, you must all have prizes," said Mr. Maynard, and so to the winning side were given boxes of candy with a funny figure of a grinning Chessy Cat on top. Both boxes and cats were bright red, and gay little prizes they were.

"But as the other side were too sad and solemn to grin broadly, we'll give them black cats," said Mr. Maynard, and all of Gladys' line received prizes exactly like the others, except that the cats were black. Of course, they were equally pretty and desirable, and were really souvenirs of the party instead of prizes.

Then they all went to the dining-room for supper. Miss Hart played a merry march on the piano, and King, escorting Gladys, went first, Marjorie and Flip followed, and then all the children came, two by two.

To carry out the idea of an "animal party," the table had been cleverly arranged to represent a farmyard. All the middle part of it was enclosed by a little fence that ran along just inside the plates, and in the enclosure were toy animals of all sorts. Downy yellow chickens, furry cats, woolly sheep, and comical roosters stood about in gay array. Also there were Teddy Bears, and possums and even lions and tigers, which though not usually found in farmyards, seemed amicably disposed enough. A delightful feast was eaten, and then, for dessert, Sarah brought in a great platter of ice cream in forms of animals. And with these animals crackers were served, and many merry jests were made as the children bit off the heads of ferocious wild beasts, or stabbed the ice cream animals with their spoons. As they left the table, each guest was invited to take one animal from the "farmyard," to carry away.

Rosy Posy announced frankly, "Don't anybuddy take de Teddy Bear, 'cause me wants it."

They all laughed, and needless to say, the bear was left for the baby, whose turn came last.

Delight chose a little white kitten, with a blue ribbon round its neck, and Gladys took a fierce-looking tiger.

Everybody agreed they had never attended a jollier party, and the smiles, as they said good-bye, were indeed of the Chessy Cat variety.

"Ourday isn't over yet, Father," said Midge, after the last guest had gone.

"Oho, I think it's time little Chessy Cats went to bed," said Mr. Maynard.

"No, indeed! the party was from four to seven, and though they staid a little later, it's only half-past seven now. And Ourday nights we always stay up till half-past eight."

"My stars! a whole hour more of Chessy Cats! That's enough to make any one grin. All right Midgety, what do you want me to do?"

"It's King's choose," said Marjorie; "it's his Ourday, you know."

So King chose "Twenty Questions," a game of which he never tired, and a jolly hour they all spent in playing it.

Then bedtime was definitely announced, and it was a lot of rather tired Chessy Cats who climbed the stairs, after many and repeated good-nights.

As Gladys' visit was to be such a short one Mrs. Maynard advised Midget not to go to lessons during her stay.

Marjorie was a little disappointed at this, but she couldn't very well go off and leave Gladys, and it would have been awkward to take her, so she staid away herself. The two girls had good times, and both Mr. and Mrs. Maynard planned many pleasant things for their enjoyment, but still Marjorie was not altogether sorry when on Tuesday Gladys took her departure.

"What's this fuss about Gladys and Delight?" asked Mr. Maynard, as they all sat chatting Tuesday evening.

"Oh, Father, it's so silly!" said Marjorie; "I don't know what to make of Delight. It isn't a bit Glad's fault. She was as sweet as pie; but Delight was as sour as buttermilk."

"She's jealous, I suppose."

"Yes, I suppose that's it. But, you see, Father, she's a different girl from us."

"Different how?"

"Oh, I don't know exactly. But she's sort of a spoiled child, you know, and whatever she has, she hates to have any one else touch it."

"Even you."

"Yes, even me. I like Delight an awful lot, but I like Gladys too."

"Of course you do. Now, Midget, listen to your old and wise Father. Forget all this foolishness. Gladys is gone now, and Delight is your very good friend, your best friend in Rockwell. Just keep on being friends with her, and do all you can to be a good friend. Don't discuss Gladys with her, don't discuss her actions, or her jealousy, or whatever foolishness is in her pretty little noddle. You are both too young to take these things seriously. But if you are a kind, loyal little friend to her, she will soon learn to be the same to you."

"But, Father, she wants me all to herself. She doesn't like to have me be friends with the other girls in Rockwell even."

"That you mustn't stand. Just go on in your own way. Be friendly with whom you choose, but always be kind and considerate of Delight's feelings. Of course, you two having your lessons alone together is largely responsible for this state of things. School would be better for you both in many ways. But you like the present arrangement, and Miss Hart is a blessing to you both. I think she can help you in persuading Delight to be a little less exacting."

"Yes, Father, she does; she understands the case, and she's always trying to make Delight less selfish."

"And perhaps,--I hate to suggest it,--but **possibly** Miss Mopsy Maynard **might** have some little tiny speck of a fault,--just a microscopic flaw in her character--"

"Now, Father, don't tease! I know I have! I'm a bad, impulsive, mischievous old thing, and I never think in time,--then the first thing I know I've done something awful! Delight's not a bit like that."

"Oh, you needn't give yourself such a dreadful character. I know you pretty well, and I'm quite pleased, on the whole, with my eldest daughter. But I do want you to learn to be a little less heedless; you know heedlessness is, after all, a sort of selfishness,--a disregard of others' convenience."

"I'm going to try, Father. I'll try real hard, and if I don't succeed, I'll try, try again."

"That's my good little Mopsy. Now, skip to bed, and don't let these serious matters keep you awake. Forget them, and dream of fairies and princesses dressed in pearls and roses and all sorts of lovely things."

"And blue velvet robes trimmed with ermine?"

"Yes, and golden sceptres, and swanboats to ride in on lakes where pond lilies bloom."

"And golden chariots, with milk white steeds, garlanded with flowers."

"Yes,--and that's about all; good-night."

"And enchanted carpets that carry you in a minute to India and Arabia."

"Yes, and upstairs to bed! Good-night."

"And knights in armor, with glittering spears--"

"Good-night, Marjorie Maynard!"

"Good-night, Father. And rose-gardens with fountains and singing birds--"

"Skip, you rascal! Scamper, fly, scoot! Good-night for the last time!"

"Good-night," called Marjorie, half way up-stairs, "good-night, Father dear."

"Good-night, Midget, good-night."

The Codes Of Hammurabi And Moses
W. W. Davies

QTY

The discovery of the Hammurabi Code is one of the greatest achievements of archaeology, and is of paramount interest, not only to the student of the Bible, but also to all those interested in ancient history...

Religion   ISBN: *1-59462-338-4*   Pages:132
MSRP $12.95

The Theory of Moral Sentiments
Adam Smith

QTY

This work from 1749. contains original theories of conscience amd moral judgment and it is the foundation for systemof morals.

Philosophy ISBN: *1-59462-777-0*   Pages:536
MSRP $19.95

Jessica's First Prayer
Hesba Stretton

QTY

In a screened and secluded corner of one of the many railway-bridges which span the streets of London there could be seen a few years ago, from five o'clock every morning until half past eight, a tidily set-out coffee-stall, consisting of a trestle and board, upon which stood two large tin cans, with a small fire of charcoal burning under each so as to keep the coffee boiling during the early hours of the morning when the work-people were thronging into the city on their way to their daily toil...

Childrens   ISBN: *1-59462-373-2*

Pages:84
MSRP $9.95

My Life and Work
Henry Ford

QTY

Henry Ford revolutionized the world with his implementation of mass production for the Model T automobile. Gain valuable business insight into his life and work with his own auto-biography... "We have only started on our development of our country we have not as yet, with all our talk of wonderful progress, done more than scratch the surface. The progress has been wonderful enough but..."

Biographies/   ISBN: *1-59462-198-5*

Pages:300
MSRP $21.95

The Art of Cross-Examination
Francis Wellman

QTY

I presume it is the experience of every author, after his first book is published upon an important subject, to be almost overwhelmed with a wealth of ideas and illustrations which could readily have been included in his book, and which to his own mind, at least, seem to make a second edition inevitable. Such certainly was the case with me; and when the first edition had reached its sixth impression in five months, I rejoiced to learn that it seemed to my publishers that the book had met with a sufficiently favorable reception to justify a second and considerably enlarged edition. ..

Reference   ISBN: *1-59462-647-2*

Pages:412

MSRP $19.95

On the Duty of Civil Disobedience
Henry David Thoreau

QTY

Thoreau wrote his famous essay, On the Duty of Civil Disobedience, as a protest against an unjust but popular war and the immoral but popular institution of slave-owning. He did more than write—he declined to pay his taxes, and was hauled off to gaol in consequence. Who can say how much this refusal of his hastened the end of the war and of slavery ?

Law   ISBN: *1-59462-747-9*

Pages:48

MSRP $7.45

Dream Psychology Psychoanalysis for Beginners
Sigmund Freud

QTY

Sigmund Freud, born Sigismund Schlomo Freud (May 6, 1856 - September 23, 1939), was a Jewish-Austrian neurologist and psychiatrist who co-founded the psychoanalytic school of psychology. Freud is best known for his theories of the unconscious mind, especially involving the mechanism of repression; his redefinition of sexual desire as mobile and directed towards a wide variety of objects; and his therapeutic techniques, especially his understanding of transference in the therapeutic relationship and the presumed value of dreams as sources of insight into unconscious desires.

Psychology   ISBN: *1-59462-905-6*

Pages:196

MSRP $15.45

The Miracle of Right Thought
Orison Swett Marden

QTY

Believe with all of your heart that you will do what you were made to do. When the mind has once formed the habit of holding cheerful, happy, prosperous pictures, it will not be easy to form the opposite habit. It does not matter how improbable or how far away this realization may see, or how dark the prospects may be, if we visualize them as best we can, as vividly as possible, hold tenaciously to them and vigorously struggle to attain them, they will gradually become actualized, realized in the life. But a desire, a longing without endeavor, a yearning abandoned or held indifferently will vanish without realization.

Pages:360

Self Help   ISBN: *1-59462-644-8*   *MSRP $25.45*

QTY

The Rosicrucian Cosmo-Conception Mystic Christianity *by Max Heindel*   ISBN: *1-59462-188-8*   **$38.95**
The Rosicrucian Cosmo-conception is not dogmatic, neither does it appeal to any other authority than the reason of the student. It is: not controversial, but is: sent forth in the, hope that it may help to clear...   New Age/Religion Pages 646

Abandonment To Divine Providence *by Jean-Pierre de Caussade*   ISBN: *1-59462-228-0*   **$25.95**
"The Rev. Jean Pierre de Caussade was one of the most remarkable spiritual writers of the Society of Jesus in France in the 18th Century. His death took place at Toulouse in 1751. His works have gone through many editions and have been republished...   Inspirational/Religion Pages 400

Mental Chemistry *by Charles Haanel*   ISBN: *1-59462-192-6*   **$23.95**
Mental Chemistry allows the change of material conditions by combining and appropriately utilizing the power of the mind. Much like applied chemistry creates something new and unique out of careful combinations of chemicals the mastery of mental chemistry...   New Age Pages 354

The Letters of Robert Browning and Elizabeth Barret Barrett 1845-1846 vol II   ISBN: *1-59462-193-4*   **$35.95**
by Robert Browning and Elizabeth Barrett   Biographies Pages 596

Gleanings In Genesis (volume I) *by Arthur W. Pink*   ISBN: *1-59462-130-6*   **$27.45**
Appropriately has Genesis been termed "the seed plot of the Bible" for in it we have, in germ form, almost all of the great doctrines which are afterwards fully developed in the books of Scripture which follow...   Religion/Inspirational Pages 420

The Master Key *by L. W. de Laurence*   ISBN: *1-59462-001-6*   **$30.95**
In no branch of human knowledge has there been a more lively increase of the spirit of research during the past few years than in the study of Psychology, Concentration and Mental Discipline. The requests for authentic lessons in Thought Control, Mental Discipline and...   New Age/Business Pages 422

The Lesser Key Of Solomon Goetia *by L. W. de Laurence*   ISBN: *1-59462-092-X*   **$9.95**
This translation of the first book of the "Lernegton" which for the first time made accessible to students of Talismanic Magic was done, after careful collation and edition, from numerous Ancient Manuscripts in Hebrew, Latin, and French...   New Age/Occult Pages 92

Rubaiyat Of Omar Khayyam *by Edward Fitzgerald*   ISBN: *1-59462-332-5*   **$13.95**
Edward Fitzgerald, whom the world has already learned, in spite of his own efforts to remain within the shadow of anonymity, to look upon as one of the rarest poets of the century, was born at Bredfield, in Suffolk, on the 31st of March, 1809. He was the third son of John Purcell...   Music Pages 172

Ancient Law *by Henry Maine*   ISBN: *1-59462-128-4*   **$29.95**
The chief object of the following pages is to indicate some of the earliest ideas of mankind, as they are reflected in Ancient Law, and to point out the relation of those ideas to modern thought.   Religion/History Pages 452

Far-Away Stories *by William J. Locke*   ISBN: *1-59462-129-2*   **$19.45**
"Good wine needs no bush, but a collection of mixed vintages does. And this book is just such a collection. Some of the stories I do not want to remain buried for ever in the museum files of dead magazine-numbers an author's not unpardonable vanity..."   Fiction Pages 272

Life of David Crockett *by David Crockett*   ISBN: *1-59462-250-7*   **$27.45**
"Colonel David Crockett was one of the most remarkable men of the times in which he lived. Born in humble life, but gifted with a strong will, an indomitable courage, and unremitting perseverance...   Biographies/New Age Pages 424

Lip-Reading *by Edward Nitchie*   ISBN: *1-59462-206-X*   **$25.95**
Edward B. Nitchie, founder of the New York School for the Hard of Hearing, now the Nitchie School of Lip-Reading, Inc, wrote "LIP-READING Principles and Practice". The development and perfecting of this meritorious work on lip-reading was an undertaking...   How-to Pages 400

A Handbook of Suggestive Therapeutics, Applied Hypnotism, Psychic Science   ISBN: *1-59462-214-0*   **$24.95**
by Henry Munro   Health/New Age/Health/Self-help Pages 376

A Doll's House: and Two Other Plays *by Henrik Ibsen*   ISBN: *1-59462-112-8*   **$19.95**
Henrik Ibsen created this classic when in revolutionary 1848 Rome. Introducing some striking concepts in playwriting for the realist genre, this play has been studied the world over.   Fiction/Classics/Plays 308

The Light of Asia *by sir Edwin Arnold*   ISBN: *1-59462-204-3*   **$13.95**
In this poetic masterpiece, Edwin Arnold describes the life and teachings of Buddha. The man who was to become known as Buddha to the world was born as Prince Gautama of India but he rejected the worldly riches and abandoned the reigns of power when...   Religion/History/Biographies Pages 170

The Complete Works of Guy de Maupassant *by Guy de Maupassant*   ISBN: *1-59462-157-8*   **$16.95**
"For days and days, nights and nights, I had dreamed of that first kiss which was to consecrate our engagement, and I knew not on what spot I should put my lips..."   Fiction/Classics Pages 240

The Art of Cross-Examination *by Francis L. Wellman*   ISBN: *1-59462-309-0*   **$26.95**
Written by a renowned trial lawyer, Wellman imparts his experience and uses case studies to explain how to use psychology to extract desired information through questioning.   How-to/Science/Reference Pages 408

Answered or Unanswered? *by Louisa Vaughan*   ISBN: *1-59462-248-5*   **$10.95**
Miracles of Faith in China   Religion Pages 112

The Edinburgh Lectures on Mental Science (1909) *by Thomas*   ISBN: *1-59462-008-3*   **$11.95**
This book contains the substance of a course of lectures recently given by the writer in the Queen Street Hall, Edinburgh. Its purpose is to indicate the Natural Principles governing the relation between Mental Action and Material Conditions...   New Age/Psychology Pages 148

Ayesha *by H. Rider Haggard*   ISBN: *1-59462-301-5*   **$24.95**
Verily and indeed it is the unexpected that happens! Probably if there was one person upon the earth from whom the Editor of this, and of a certain previous history, did not expect to hear again...   Classics Pages 380

Ayala's Angel *by Anthony Trollope*   ISBN: *1-59462-352-X*   **$29.95**
The two girls were both pretty, but Lucy who was twenty-one who supposed to be simple and comparatively unattractive, whereas Ayala was credited, as her Bombwhat romantic name might show, with poetic charm and a taste for romance. Ayala when her father died was nineteen...   Fiction Pages 484

The American Commonwealth *by James Bryce*   ISBN: *1-59462-286-8*   **$34.45**
An interpretation of American democratic political theory. It examines political mechanics and society from the perspective of Scotsman James Bryce   Politics Pages 572

Stories of the Pilgrims *by Margaret P. Pumphrey*   ISBN: *1-59462-116-2*   **$17.95**
This book explores pilgrims religious oppression in England as well as their escape to Holland and eventual crossing to America on the Mayflower, and their early days in New England...   History Pages 268

www.bookjungle.com *email: sales@bookjungle.com fax: 630-214-0564 mail: Book Jungle PO Box 2226 Champaign, IL 61825*

QTY

The Fasting Cure *by Sinclair Upton* ISBN: *1-59462-222-1* **$13.95**
In the Cosmopolitan Magazine for May, 1910, and in the Contemporary Review (London) for April, 1910, I published an article dealing with my experiences in fasting. I have written a great many magazine articles, but never one which attracted so much attention... New Age/Self Help/Health Pages 164

Hebrew Astrology *by Sepharial* ISBN: *1-59462-308-2* **$13.45**
In these days of advanced thinking it is a matter of common observation that we have left many of the old landmarks behind and that we are now pressing forward to greater heights and to a wider horizon than that which represented the mind-content of our progenitors... Astrology Pages 144

Thought Vibration or The Law of Attraction in the Thought World ISBN: *1-59462-127-6* **$12.95**
by William Walker Atkinson *Psychology/Religion Pages 144*

Optimism *by Helen Keller* ISBN: *1-59462-108-X* **$15.95**
Helen Keller was blind, deaf, and mute since 19 months old, yet famously learned how to overcome these handicaps, communicate with the world, and spread her lectures promoting optimism. An inspiring read for everyone... Biographies/Inspirational Pages 84

Sara Crewe *by Frances Burnett* ISBN: *1-59462-360-0* **$9.45**
In the first place, Miss Minchin lived in London. Her home was a large, dull, tall one, in a large, dull square, where all the houses were alike, and all the sparrows were alike, and where all the door-knockers made the same heavy sound... Childrens/Classic Pages 88

The Autobiography of Benjamin Franklin *by Benjamin Franklin* ISBN: *1-59462-135-7* **$24.95**
The Autobiography of Benjamin Franklin has probably been more extensively read than any other American historical work, and no other book of its kind has had such ups and downs of fortune. Franklin lived for many years in England, where he was agent... Biographies/History Pages 332

Name	
Email	
Telephone	
Address	
City, State ZIP	

☐ **Credit Card**   ☐ **Check / Money Order**

Credit Card Number	
Expiration Date	
Signature	

Please Mail to: Book Jungle
PO Box 2226
Champaign, IL 61825
or Fax to: 630-214-0564

ORDERING INFORMATION
web: *www.bookjungle.com*
email: *sales@bookjungle.com*
fax: *630-214-0564*
mail: *Book Jungle PO Box 2226 Champaign, IL 61825*
or PayPal *to sales@bookjungle.com*

Please contact us for bulk discounts

DIRECT-ORDER TERMS

**20% Discount if You Order
Two or More Books**
Free Domestic Shipping!
Accepted: Master Card, Visa,
Discover, American Express

www.ingramcontent.com/pod-product-compliance
Lightning Source LLC
Chambersburg PA
CBHW080909020726
47502CB00008B/2400